Taking Liberties
A Short Story Anthology

Breakthrough Books

First published in Great Britain in 2023 by Breakthrough Books.

Paperback ISBN: 978-1-7393793-0-8

The rights of Stephanie Bretherton, Jamie Chipperfield, Sue Clark, Jason Cobley, Stevyn Colgan, Samuel Dodson, A.B. Kyazze, Virginia Moffatt, Ivy Ngeow, Eamon Somers, Paul Waters and PJ Whiteley, to be identified as the authors of this Work have been asserted by them in accordance with the Copyright, Designs and Patents Act 1988.

Copyright © 2023

All rights reserved.

No part of this book may be reproduced in any form or by any electronic or mechanical means, including information storage and retrieval systems, without written permission from the author, except for the use of brief quotations in a book review.

This book is a work of fiction and semi-fiction. Names, characters, places and incidents are either a product of the authors' imagination or are used fictitiously. Any resemblance to actual people, living or dead, events or locales is entirely coincidental. Written in both UK and US English, this book retains the original language of the stories and voices of the individual authors.

Contents

Foreword	v
1. HUMAN ERROR Stephanie Bretherton	1
2. EUTIERRIA Jason Cobley	17
3. MEDIUM WELL DONE Stevyn Colgan	28
4. THE LAST APPOINTMENT Virginia Moffatt	44
5. SNUFFR Paul Waters	53
6. SEIZE YOUR FREEDOM WITH BOTH HANDS A.B. Kyazze	61
7. FREE TO LIE IN BED AS IF WAKING-UP-TIME WILL NEVER COME Eamon Somers	65
8. THE HERMIT Samuel Dodson	70
9. FLUID DYNAMICS Ivy Ngeow	77
10. ON THE BRUSHES Sue Clark	86
11. MAGNOLIA WALLS Jamie Chipperfield	93
12. GRINGOS CAN'T DANCE PJ Whiteley	99

Before you go	115
About the authors	117
Acknowledgments	121

Foreword

What price freedom? Much debated by philosophers, politicians, activists and poets alike, the concept is particular to each individual despite common fundamentals. To the writer, freedom has its own flavour and resonance.

Those of us who cannot help but wrangle words onto a page often feel bound by this compulsion, while straining against whatever keeps us from living this call as purely and freely as we can. Yet we plough on in hope, creating make-believe despite the pressures of everyday reality (from the day job to the publishing market) simply because we must.

When asked to supply a story for an anthology loosely based on the notion of freedom, the 12 authors included here applied their unique style, interests and imagination to producing pieces as varied as they are vivid.

The *Breakthrough Books* collective was thus born, and *Taking Liberties* is its first offering.

An informal affiliation of writerly colleagues from diverse backgrounds, the collective members came to know each other, initially online, through the ups and downs of publishing our novels. We befriended, backed, supported and cheered each other on through the process of book-making at every stage. While our chosen genres may differ, we have read and appreciated each other's work and share many values both as authors and humans. (Nothing here was composed by a bot!)

It has been a joy and an honour to work together in creating *Taking Liberties*. There's plenty more to come from this nascent publishing venture, so we very much hope you enjoy our first offering.

The *Breakthrough Books* collective

"When I let go of what I am, I become what I might be."

— Lao Tzu

Human Error
Stephanie Bretherton

Henry watched her from the deck, knowing she wouldn't mind. Knowing the way she'd walked the longer route around the terrace towards the deep end, the way she'd slowly unpeeled her silk sarong meant she wanted him to watch. How had he come to be so blessed?

This rare gift of love, his ability to truly appreciate it, had not been purchased by Sandy's beauty alone. Or by how readily and skilfully she met his particular needs. The feeling Henry relished most was the satisfaction of being appreciated in return. For all that he was, for all that he could do for her. And she was grateful, his Sandy. Not simply for what he gave her (and she deserved every pretty little thing that he bestowed upon her, he often told her so) but for him. Sandy was thankful to be loved by him.

This was not the kind of gratitude that came with the middle-aged mail-order bride his grandfather had taken on his semi-senility. Sandy could have had anyone, done anything she set her mind to. She had not been chosen from a catalogue. His beloved had been chosen, yes, but not in that way.

Sipping his vintage Japanese whiskey, Henry watched her as she walked toward the diving board, the one he had designed and printed for her. He admired her hip-rolling gait, a family trait that came from one leg growing slightly longer than the other. (He had not corrected that.) He enjoyed the way this gorgeous imperfection sent a ripple up her yoga-supple spine and onwards through the waving flag of her long red hair. Her natural, blood-orange hair.

But then, everything about Sandy was natural, no synth glitches, no blank-eyed acquiescence. Henry had no respect for those idiots who wrote such inane qualities into their code, into their dull and useless fakes. Did they not understand? It was the right degree of manageable flaw that made a woman interesting.

Henry adored the red-headed cliché of Sandy's scalding temper – another expression, he believed, of the gene responsible for painting in her unforgettable colouring. Sometimes, he would deliberately annoy her, if only to ignite the fireworks in her blue-green eyes, if only to make it up to her afterwards. He could always calm her into a state of more malleable excitability. This trick was no accident. Henry took pride in the bespoke curriculum of nurture that had soothed and balanced the innate volatility of her nature. He'd done his homework, invested in the optimum conditions.

Why skimp? Generosity was in *his* nature, and he'd never been short of funds. Sandy was his first, and a prize for sure, but he had refused to repeat her for anyone else. That would not have been right, and not only for selfish reasons. He loved her too much to risk her happiness, to ever let her come face-to-face with an animated likeness. Sandy did not know, after all.

The acceleration process had been risky, but there'd been enough time to imprint the charade of memory that kept her happy and well-adjusted, made her his. He'd been content to wait for the right moment to introduce himself, patience being another of his virtues.

If he was honest, those weren't the primary reasons Sandy's source DNA was vaulted. Not simply to keep her stable, or special. There would be another danger in commonality. Alex. But she was miles away now, married, and blissful in her ignorance. What he possessed today far surpassed anything they could have built together, and he was convinced they would have long since divorced, even if she *had* said yes. Alex's faults had not been so easily managed.

'WELL, HOLY SHIT. THE WEIRDEST THING.'

'What, my love?'

'You don't have a younger sister do you?'

'Don't be ridiculous, you know I don't? This from the man who blames my every issue on my so-called only-child syndrome!'

'No, no, of course. Well, I guess it's true then. We do all have a doppelganger somewhere.'

'What are you talking about?'

'Her. This girl.'

Alex gasped as Luca showed her his device and zoomed in for a grainy close-up.

'My God.'

Alex wanted to be excited, to enjoy the thrill of the bizarre, but a ball of nausea deep in her belly told her a truth she could not accept. She was looking at herself.

SANDY'S DIVE WAS PERFECT. She parted the water with no splash, barely a ripple. Her hair slicked into a dark rope behind her as she emerged at the other end after only three strokes and a single breath. She leaned over the infinity edge as she loved to do, meditating on the horizon and merging, from Henry's perspective, with the deep, silent, navy lake behind.

He had not allowed her to abandon her talent as Alex had done. Alex could have been an Olympian (Sandy too, if such a public profile had been possible) but she had chosen her NGO calling instead. Over everything she could have had, all that she could have been. Sandy's gifts were not to be cast aside so easily. Nor cut short, like Alex's hair, for the practicality of travel and playing doctors and nurses in some godforsaken refugee camp.

Diving practice was daily, lessons came weekly – Sandy's schedule was carefully controlled. She had no idea this was so, or that it was unlike any other woman's. Henry was no tyrant, however. Sandy had the freedom to work and she had chosen to keep working for him (it would have been criminal to let that brain go to waste.)

She engineered medical robotics as part of a small, hand-picked team located off-site in a biometrically secure lab, two miles from home. Between the lab and the villa was a shopping mall, a cinema, a bowling alley, a holocourt, but Henry had arranged for her to shop and play out of hours with her bodyguard, Delilah, whom Sandy thought was her best friend.

Delilah was not the only security. There was a more visible presence to throw Sandy off the scent of that particular subterfuge. His darling now understood (ever since the staged kidnap attempt) that precautions were necessary.

Henry smiled at the memory of his performance that night, as he'd dropped to his knees before her to apologise for such appalling trauma on his account. This was the curse of being with a wealthy man, he had said with bitter regret, a man with sensitive government contracts. He would understand, of course, if she wanted to leave. Of course, she had not.

Why would she? They went to dinner in restaurants he owned, filled with discreet, well-paid actors. He threw lavish parties at home, where phones were collected together with coats at the door. Sandy had personal masseurs, beauticians, fitness classes in the pool house gym.

She remained under the care of the therapist she'd been seeing at his expense since their first date (when Henry had been suitably shocked and saddened to learn, during a champagne hover globe tour of the canyon, that her parents had died the year before in a freak shuttle crash.) He was excellent value, that charlatan shrink who remained completely clueless, especially about the fact that every session was recorded.

Sandy was a passable twenty-six (ten) when Henry had orchestrated physically 'bumping' into her, with precision timing to make this a physical actuality. Her mortification about the coffee she'd spilled down the boss's pristine shirt impelled her to accept a date, despite her better (or suggested) judgement.

Now officially thirty, she'd probably look more like forty were it not for the subtle intervention, which at this stage was more cosmetic than cellular. He didn't know how much longer that would hold back the fast-forwarded years, but he had another Sandy in preparation, just in case.

Her template, Alex, was fifty now and looked amazing, even without the work he knew she would have refused. He'd seen her in a news item recently. So, even if Sandy soon appeared that age she would still be stunning, still be sexy and hormone replacement should take care of the rest. As long as there was no decline in cognition. A few character lines he could handle, even a little sag, but dementia would be the deal-breaker.

An incurable and fast-spreading cancer would be called upon in that event. One that gave them enough time for the most poignant of farewells... and to prepare the spare. He was also testing a new RNA snip and splice delivery system to import the epigenetic tags that Sandy1 had acquired during their life together, in case they carried some capacity to more quickly recognise or re-express her love for him – and to appropriately respond to his.

Next time, he didn't want to have to work so hard. Not all over again. His patented ReJuve8 continued to react beautifully within his own cells, rebuilding the telomeres, but nevertheless at ninety, he was feeling a little tired.

Alex needed more vodka. Her pulse had spiked, her mind was wading through a swamp of bewilderment.

'Where did you take this picture?'

'I didn't. Someone sent it to me, a guy who'd seen you on my screensaver.'

'Who?'

'A sales rep for that suture drone we've just bought for the field hospital.'

'Christ. Where did he take it?'

'Some ultra-secure lab up in the mountains – he doesn't even know where... get this, they were taken there for training in a fleet of hovers with the windows blacked out 360!'

Her stomach tightened. She knew the answer to her next question but asked it anyway, a wave of rage rising to its crest.

'Who makes the drone?'

'TheraZerve. I think they're a subsidiary of...'

'HyLyve.'

'Yeah, how did you ...'

'I know where she is, Luca. And I know who made her.'

'What?'

Sandy wasn't feeling well. This had been happening more and more but she hadn't wanted to upset Henry. He did so worry about her. But despite the nausea and the tiredness she had dragged herself to work, there was a big order to fulfil and she couldn't let anyone down. Big orders concerned Sandy more than they should.

Of course, she wanted the business to be successful, but a large consignment usually meant someone, somewhere was planning a military intervention. She wanted her little doctors to do their job well but she was sad about why they were needed. With ground engagement between bio forces now so rare, the casualties were largely collateral.

She stayed a while longer after everyone had gone. Told Delilah not to wait, to go on home, almost had to push her out the door. Henry would send Armando when she was ready. The entire auto-fleet was busy ferrying people to and from some press event he was holding at the main site. If only she had learned to drive herself, she could have taken one of the retro manual vehicles that Henry collected, but the fits had deprived her of that freedom.

THE CLONED WIG was a work of art, the prosthetic nose miraculous, the replica irises astonishing. Even Luca did a double-take. The guards at the camp could detect no anomalies as she walked through the screening cube. They didn't ask her why she needed to test this strange costume. Alex saved lives at the risk of her own, this was all they needed to know.

Luca's cousin, Anna-Maria, had couriered her own press credentials along with a few strands of her hair, the follicles still fresh. She shared enough of Alex's rage, once enlightened, to share in this risk.

THE TRIP out to the compound was as bizarre as Alex had expected and her heart rate did nothing to ease the sense of unreality. She was thankful for all those mindfulness sessions, for the Krav Maga, for any coping mechanism that allowed her to rein back the fury, the disgust, and every avenging angel of this violation.

Press were allowed only as far as the media centre but tonight the Perseids were due, and considering the nocturnal clarity of their location, special dispensation had been given for a reception on the viewing platform.

Alex knew where and how to get underneath that – and where to go from there. But she knew she had to get out before Henry made his grand entrance. The ruse had proved successful so far, but she felt that somehow he would know she was there, that he would smell her, sense her presence.

Would "Anna-Maria" be missed? Maybe, but where would they think to look first? Not the humble medi-drone lab. That was all for PR, a hobby to make him feel better about himself. Henry had bigger intellectual property to protect, juicier rumours to deny.

The first meteors began to slice through the blackness and the guests whispered and gasped their excitement. Everyone was a child once more under the pyrotechnics of the night sky. And then, exactly as Alex had hoped, the lights were dimmed to enhance the view. This was her moment. Now.

WAS THAT SOMEONE BEHIND HER? She stopped, crouched behind a shrub, trying to silence the deafening bass beats of her heart so she could listen, deeply. The twist and crunch of all that loose mountain shale underfoot had done her few favours.

It was no one. An animal maybe, her imagination more likely. Alex realised that the crouch she was in was not the best position, too hard from here to overpower one of Henry's goons. The sense of being followed might have come from a sentry hawk on a pre-programmed circuit, but if it *had* picked her up and pinged back an alert it was too late now. She was committed. The hike so far had been harder than she remembered, despite all her training, but better to keep moving. Fast.

She was breathless when she approached the lab so stopped to allow her temperature to normalise, conscious of any heat sensors at the perimeter. She removed the wig, the nose, the contact lens, pulled on the Therma-BLOC hood and gloves and rested a while.

There were no obvious signs of a human security detail, they must all be reassigned to the press event. On any other day, Henry might have been justified in trusting his biometric tech, it was the best in the business, after all. Unless, of course, an intruder's DNA was an exact match for one of the facility's employees.

SHE HAD ANTICIPATED HAVING to hide somewhere, hole up until morning. Recalling the janitorial store in the restrooms at ground level, Alex hoped it might have the same combination. Henry would have changed every staff member who had known her – well before positioning the 'replacement' – but he had a few stubborn quirks and lucky numbers were among them.

Alex turned down a long half-lit corridor, confidently, as if she belonged, not sure if anyone would still be around. Everything seemed eased down for the night, deserted. So to walk right into her as she was coming out of the restroom was heart-stopping.

Each stood still, staring at the other for a moment. If Sandy had recognised her she didn't show it yet. Alex's own hair was pixie cropped these days, but still the same unmistakable shade. Her own eyes, for all the laughter lines beneath, were looking back at her from a perfect, younger reflection. Alex wanted to cry but clenched her jaw until she'd bullied it back.

'Oh, gosh, sorry, I didn't know anyone else was here still. Who... um, I'm sorry, who are you?'

Her voice. Not the way Alex heard it in her head, but the same bright tone that she knew greeted callers when they missed her in person and got her answering message instead. She shivered.

'I'm Alex. Hello Sandy.'

'Oh, have we met? Sorry, I'm a little confused, you look familiar but I can't place you? Are you here for the event? If so, you're in the wrong place...'

'I'm here for you.'

Something shifted in Sandy's eyes, her posture softened, she swayed a little. Yes. Her body knew, her cells knew, even if the revelation had not yet percolated to conscious understanding.

'Wait. I know you. Wait – are we related?'

Sandy searched her false memory.

'Come back into the restroom with me for a moment, please.'

Sandy followed, meekly, hypnotically.

'Stand next to me and look in the mirror. Please, try to trust me. Just look for a while.'

Their height was an exact match. Minutes lost shape and meaning as each woman looked, and looked, in silence.

Finally, Sandy began to weep. Huge, slow-rolling drops of uncomprehending grief.

'Oh. God.'

She started to shake and Alex took her in her arms, wrapped her in all the lost and lonely years of their separate childhoods. She held back her own urge to wail and sob, this broken girl needed all her strength now and she would give her nothing less.

Then a shock. Suddenly, Sandy was pushing her away with violence, eyes ablaze, brows contracting into a vicious scowl. Alex had never seen herself angry before – and now she understood why it frightened some.

'Why! Why would you do this to me? You could have just left me, left me as I was. I was happy.'

'Were you? Really?'

'Whoever you are, I think you only want to hurt us. Yes, that's it, you're jealous! Henry told me most women would be jealous of me. If he didn't love you anymore, if you got too old, that's not my fault!'

She was a child. A confused little girl whose toys had been taken, whose best friend had chosen another, who'd been scolded and taken home early from the party. A child in a woman's body.

'Sandy, I know this is hard... crazy, unreal. But you're angry with the wrong person. You see, it was I that left Henry – and that's why he made you. He took my DNA, Sandy, our DNA, without my permission. And that's why he hides you away. He broke the law, he broke every regulation and principle. He broke both our hearts. I'm so, so sorry, but you've been living in a fantasy. Henry's fantasy.'

Alex moved closer again.

'I thought long and hard about what this might do to you, but I kept coming back to the conviction that, as hard as it hurts, I would have wanted to know. I, you, we. All I had to go on were my instincts, Sandy. Some of those are probably yours too. I don't know. I don't know you, and yet I do. And I know I would have wanted to be free from any cage, no matter how cosy, how pretty. That's why I left him in the first place. That's why I had no choice but to unlock yours.'

She reached out to touch Sandy's arm.

'You're in shock. I know, I understand. You're scared, you're angry, you're confused. I get that. But you're also much stronger than you know, no matter what he's told you, or made you feel. I'll take care of you, Sandy. There's a whole world out there for you. It might be broken and bleeding in too many places, but there's still so much for you to see, to experience, to discover for yourself. For real this time. This is all just a diamond-tipped lie, it's all an illusion.'

Sandy's breath was easing, her fists untangling.

'Maybe I liked my illusion.'

'No. You can't have. You've felt trapped every day that you've been with him. I know you, Sandy. I am you.'

'Oh God. I think maybe I've always known. I dream about you, you know. No, not you but someone who looks a lot like you. Nothing like the mother he gave me.'

'Yes, that would be right. No one was like our mother. She was one of a kind. Unlike us. Ha! No, I'm sorry, that's not funny. And I'm sorry that you never knew her. Really, so sorry.'

Sandy was still now. Eyes seeking into her sister's.

'So. What now? What are we going to do? He won't ever let me go, you know.'

'We'll see. I have a few secret weapons in my arsenal when it comes to Henry.'

HENRY DID NOT SEEM surprised to see her. To see them both, side by side. Armando came out onto the deck, perplexed but de-holstered and ready. Henry waved him away.

'Ah. So, it was you. The missing journalist. Clever, Alex, very clever. Naturally.'

'You did a good job, Henry. Amazing for such a short time span. Except that she's a much better person than me. I wanted to kill you, she just wants you to say you're sorry.'

'For what? To her, for what? I gave her life, I gave her everything. I love her.'

Henry looked at Sandy now.

'I love you, you know that, Baby.'

Alex moved in front of Sandy.

'Apologise to me then. You stole from me, Henry. In the worst possible way. You're a thief, an abuser, a liar.'

Henry spoke through her.

'Sandy, you are everything that your twin here isn't. I made you so much better. You'll hate each other, you know.'

Alex moved back and took Sandy's hand.

'Don't believe him Sandy, he's a living lie. He's so convincing because he believes it all himself. Oh yeah, great pool, by the way, Henry. It's the one I told you about in my dream, isn't it? The one I drew for you? And I'm sure Sandy loves it too, but you know what, it turns out that DNA is thicker than water. Or, at least than your facsimile of love. Sandy is coming with me, Henry, and you're going to let her go.'

Henry smiled, exhaled.

'She won't survive long without me, you know. You think you're on some kind of mercy mission, delivering justice, but you've only scorched the earth and poisoned the well. The acceleration can't be stopped but it can be managed and I've got everything in place to take care of her when she starts to decline. You may think you're getting a sister or a daughter, Alex, but you'll end up with your grandmother before too long.'

The bile burst into the back of her throat. Alex had never wanted to break her Hippocratic Oath before. Never wanted to do anything or anyone more harm.

She felt Sandy sway again as she took in the understanding of her limited lifespan. Alex squeezed her hand, gave her what strength she could spare. She wanted to hold her again, as she had done for almost an hour in the darkness outside the lab, as they had talked and watched the heavenly shower overhead, but she couldn't give Henry the advantage. Not now.

'Nice, Henry. Really, nice work. You must be so proud of yourself. Well. At least she'll be free until then.'

'She's free now. She could've walked away at any time, but she chose to stay.'

'She chose to stay in a lie because it was the only truth she knew. You need to whistle up one of your hovers, Henry. We're leaving now.'

Alex began to back away, but then stopped as a sudden question pressed its way into her plans. The answer to which might change everything. Might demand a more measured approach and the reigning in of her fury.

'Oh no, wait... wait a minute. That's not all, is it Henry?'

She cocked her head and looked at him with hard, cold determination as the realisation dawned.

'I want the other one too.'

'What other one?' Henry shrugged, trying to smile.

'Don't tell me you don't have another one, especially considering the news you've just given us about Sandy. I want her too, Henry. I want the other one.'

'She's not finished yet. You can't look after her.'

'How old is she?'

'Four, going on ten.'

'Who is she with?'

'The same family, they're on my team.'

'Then they're as bad as you and she's better off with me. With us.

You can have your quacks attend to both of them while they're with me, but you need to bring the other one here in a hover now. If you want any of this to stay quiet.'

Alex flinched as Henry began to move, but he walked away from her and over to the bar to pour more of his priceless whiskey. Then he signalled Armando who stepped from the shadows, tense and quiet.

'What will you tell her, Alex, the little one, as you take her from everything she's known? What will you tell everyone else about your sudden sisterhood?'

She thought on her feet.

'We'll work it out. I mean, I could say that she's had an illness, the same one her real mother and father died from. That she's been cared for here to get her better but now she can come and live with her sisters. Yes... because we're all no longer contagious. She's smart enough to get that right? And her fosters, for their bloody sins, can even come with us for a while.'

'Might work. But what about everyone else, Alex? What will you tell them?'

She had the finish line in her sights now and she ran with her idea.

'I'll hide her in plain sight, Henry. I'll embellish on the truth. Most people know I was IVF, I've never held that back. But now, I'll add a little extra. I'll say there was a three-way split and the other frozen embryos were donated when my parents died. I'll say I found both of them orphaned in the camps, cared for by de facto foster parents. I'll make it work. And you know that I can. I'll do everything to make it work.'

Henry shook his head.

'You could always improvise, my love. But you should know that I have six shooters trained on you right now, on both of you. I don't *need* to let anyone walk out of here.'

Alex felt Sandy's terror again, like a scalpel through her own flesh.

'People know that I'm here, Henry, and they know why.'

'You're not the only creative one, Alex. I could come up with any scenario. Cover my tracks.'

'But you won't.'

'Why?'

She saw his face, his eyes as he looked at her with such longing, as he always had done. And now she knew she had him.

'Because then you'll have to accept what an evil bastard you really are and you can't face that mirror, Henry. Even if you could, you wouldn't, because your one mistake – your one human error – has been to love too much, too hungrily. And if you want any shred of the love we both once felt for you to survive, you're going to let us go. All of us.'

Alex felt the same calm courage, the same realisation now arise in her sister. Sandy confirmed this by untangling from their clasping handhold and moving towards Henry. She looked at him, perhaps trying to see him for the first time. Then she leaned in and kissed him on the cheek.

'Goodbye, Henry.'

She eased off her enormous emerald ring and dropped it into his glass.

He crumpled. The crystal clinked as it fell from his hands, spilled its contents and rolled back toward the bar. Armando moved in to lift him up.

'Ah fuck it, this is all too hard now. I'm tired, Armando. Neither of them is worth it. Not really. Let them go. Do whatever they want. Just get them out of here.'

Suddenly, Henry looked all of his years. But Sandy was doing so much better than Alex expected, managing to lock down both her anguish and her empathy. Alex recognised the signs, but was unmoved, at least about Henry. She had said goodbye to him once before. It had flayed away a sliver of her heart at the time, but she hadn't suffered a moment's regret since fully embracing that freedom.

'Maybe you can give up the bullshit now, Henry? This pursuit of the perfect love and its absolute possession. Just give it up. If you really must have a real woman in your life then make it an honest transaction. If you can't find genuinely requited love then hire a hooker, or bring over a mail-order bride from some impoverished country, like your grandfather did. Hey, why not choose a Brit this time? I hear a lot of them are looking for alternative passports these days, and you do love that accent, don't you? Go get your things, Sandy. Whatever you want or need from here. Go on, it's ok. I'll come with you if you want?'

Sandy seemed emptied now, a rag doll with the stuffing removed, a vacuum which Alex would dedicate whatever lifetime either had left to filling with real self, real love.

'No. It's ok. I'm good, thank you, Alex. I don't need anything from here. Not a single pretty little thing.'

Eutierria
Or Becoming One With Nature
Jason Cobley

P arking the car is easy. The crunch of gravel under the tyres alerts the dog to where we are. She starts whimpering, stands up on the back seat, pacing from side to side. If she could open the door herself, she would. Unlike the kids, who would sit there and demand that the chauffeur open the door for them no matter what. I climb out, gathering up my phone, keys, and big old stick with a groove in it for my thumb. I make sure nothing is showing on the seats or footwells that would make anyone want to break into the car. I flatter myself that my Porcupine Tree CDs would be of any interest to passing would-be thieves and tuck them out of sight. I walk around to the door on the other side to let the dog out. She lets out a little excited bark as I take just that little too long to pull the handle. When I do open the door, she bounces down and immediately heads over to the undergrowth for an investigatory sniff.

'Wait,' I say, so she waits. I clip her lead on to her harness, lock the car, and we're off.

It's still early. The woods are cool, especially today, when the air is still, and the sun has yet to burn through the clouds. The dog loves it here, in as much as you can say a dog loves anything. I entertain the idea that she has complex emotions, but in truth she is driven by smells, of which there are plenty here. If I left her here, abandoned, I wonder how long it would take before she exhausted the novelty of new smells and squirrels to chase and started pining for home. Dogs adapt, but I suppose she's too domesticated to go back to the wild and live in the woods. I wonder if I could do it.

We take the path off the layby. The dog trots ahead, snuffling the hedgerows. She selects a spot to take a piss and crouches down. She must have been hanging on since before we left the house, because it takes a minute to finish. Panting a smile, she's pleased with her achievement. I congratulate her with a scratch behind the ears and an enthusiastic tummy rub, and encourage her to run on, which she does, checking every so often that I'm following. My knee is hurting today, so the stick helps. It's a useful height so I can lean my weight on it without falling over or worrying my fat bulk will cause it to snap. I'm not that fat I suppose, just averagely overweight for my age, and not as fit as I should be, what with the high blood pressure and everything else.

The trees are a contorted canopy above us, trunks split and twisted back around each other. It's a reassuring tangle, like fingers crossed over each other, hands forming an arch the way you do when you're making out that you're thinking really hard. These arboreal bouncers stand guard around the clearing, eyeing me up and down, assessing whether I'm permitted entry, whether my membership has expired, whether I look like the right clientele. They wave the dog through regardless, so I suppose I get to go in as her guest.

It's almost enough to make you forget your worries. The dog takes off after a movement in the bushes. Whether it's a real squirrel or an imagined one doesn't matter; she's off. As she crashes around, I look up at the canopy of trees, nothing swaying as there is no breeze. The nearest tree is like a set of conjoined triplets. A long time ago, either the trunk got split by lightning from a great and magic axe wielded by a Norse god, or three trees liked each other very much and decided to live entwined for the rest of their lives. Whichever it is, it starts as one tree but then, about a foot off the ground, three separate trunks have grown upwards and upwards. The upper branches intertwine in places, but the lower ones have been lopped neatly: someone has been round with a saw. Three trees bound together for all eternity.

I used to think that would be me: bound to another soul until I end up rooted in the ground myself. I was proved wrong. Ten years ago today, I lost Carol. Marriage wasn't forever, even though we'd both promised. You can make a promise, you can even mean it, but in the end it doesn't make any difference if there are other plans in place. The last couple of years with my second wife Clare have been hard. Her bloody kids. That's another reason why I got this dog, so I've got an excuse to get out of the house. It's just me and the dog, with the air and the quiet, and every now and then, we come to these woods.

The dog bounds back towards me, with no prize from her miniature hunting expedition other than a lolling tongue and a wagging tail. From this clearing, there are three paths: one continues the well-worn path we were on, taking a circuitous route around the wood back to the road; another does similar but heads the other way; the third is the proverbial less-trodden, criss-crossed with fallen boughs and dips that flood when it rains. You can guess which one the dog takes. I let her choose. I've got legs. I can climb over things and muddy boots can be cleaned. Besides, it might take a bit longer and then I won't feel the need to rush back to the house and Clare's kids with their phones, consoles, busy screens, and blank stares.

I've lost sight of the dog. She's tramping through brambles, diving after wriggling and rustling things on the forest floor like an electric strimmer, so I can hear her. I can't follow the sound exactly, as I have to step over a fallen tree to get to her. The tree's bark has yet to be ravaged by moss and insects, so its fall must be relatively recent. I'm not going to investigate its roots, but two thirds of the way along its length, it bisects like a pair of legs. Its crotch mysterious and blank, each leg has grown to escape the other one. The lower one has succumbed to weight and is reclining on the ground. The upper one seemingly already had a life of its own before it fell, branching off again. Each branch is now buried in the green masses of another tree, one that I suspect is singularly unimpressed with having to break the fall.

I wonder how much trees are even aware of each other. I know there are theories, both outlandish and scientific, but it would be good to know whether they have some sort of telepathy or whether they live their long lives languishing inside themselves like we do. I don't know what I'd do with that information, mind. It would be terrifying to know what trees are thinking when we climb them, cut them down or, worse, when my dog pisses against them.

The dog's head pops up and I can see where she is. I sit on the fallen trunk, then swivel around, swinging my legs over as best I can. I'm too old to get over any other way. There was a time, of course, when I'd take a running jump and clear it easily but I'm certainly not fifteen anymore. She sees me and comes bounding back for some approbation, which of course she gets. I rub her head, fuss her behind the ears, and she's happy. She's looking for a dog treat. She knows they're in my pocket but I'm saving them for when I need to bribe her to get back into the car later. I wave her on and she trots off again, with me following along the brambly path. I could almost do this all day.

The path through the woods is cool. The morning sun is starting to come through, but we're still shielded, in our leafy cocoon. It's such a relief to be out and about without sweltering after five minutes. Last week's heatwave was too much, the hottest it's been for years. I think they said on the news that one day last week was the hottest on record. We kept the curtains drawn and the windows closed. With Clare working from home, I had to come clean and tell her about my job, that I'd taken garden leave. It was mutual, I said. I'll get another job no problem, I said. She just looked at me and didn't need to say anything to make me feel like a selfish piece of shit. But, today, that's the least of my worries. Bruce Springsteen's *Lonesome Day* runs through my head, and I hum the chorus as I hack at the tangled vegetation at my feet with my stick.

I suppose I am feeling lonesome, if that's the right word. There just doesn't seem to be much to show for a lived life after all this time. I've stacked up a few experiences, sure, but have I achieved all that much in my fifty years? I had a first marriage that didn't end in a way anybody could have predicted, a few years inside myself and working a job that is making me obsolete, and now a second marriage that is waning in a way everybody should have predicted. The dog and I get on fine, but dogs are pretty resilient. They might get attached to a person, but take that away and they'll just transfer their affections to whoever's feeding them every day.

I wonder if the dog would miss me at all if I just turned around and left her here. I wonder whether I'd be missed at home if I drove off and never came back. Sometimes, it feels like the right course of action, the thing to do, but I don't know where I'd end up, probably driving up and down the motorway in an endless, aimless loop. Besides, I wouldn't be here to see the dog taking a shit behind a log like she is now. I take a look but it's too messy to pick up easily, so I kick some forest floor detritus over it to hide it, like a little tomb, a tiny barrow for an ancient chieftain made of dogshit. A clump of mushrooms, dark-helmeted and shiny, stand guard like riot policemen over the little memorial to my dog's defecation. She pads off again and I follow, steadying myself with the stick. My knee is just about managing.

When I was young, aged about ten or eleven, there were some woods near our house. They backed out onto some army barracks, and there was a tramp who lived in the woods. He had built himself a bivouac that he augmented, over the years, with a proper bed, bolstered roof, and even a little library. He was set up on the edge of a little clearing and had a fire on the go almost constantly so he could boil water for his tea, cook his food, and have a little warmth. My friends and I would pedal up there on our Raleigh Chopper bikes and visit him. A couple of them took the piss and only came the once, but my mate Greg and I went a bit more often. I don't even remember his name now, but the tramp must have been around my age now, and the story was that he'd been discharged from the army but had nowhere to go, so he camped down in the woods. The army knew he was there, the local police knew he was there, most of the kids in the area knew he was there, but no one much cared. He did no harm, we thought. We'd sit and make toast on his fire and listen to him tell rambling, semi-coherent stories, all the time lying on his mattress in his makeshift tent whilst we did wheelies around the campfire.

I don't live around there anymore. When I first moved down this way, it was just weeks after Carol's funeral. I sold the house as quickly as I could. We didn't have kids, so it was easy, straightforward. My buyer was a first-timer and I wasn't buying anything else, so it was done quickly. I came down here, rented a flat and got a job that paid the bills. I'd lost all ambition when she died. That was when I got my first dog and discovered the woods. He and I would come here at least once a week, even when it was chucking it down with rain or the snow painted the trees and plastered the ground. He lasted a good few years, even though he was a good age when I got him from the rescue centre. When I had to send him off, I sat in the vet's waiting room for an hour and wept more than I had when Carol died. I eventually got replacements for both.

I had been on my own for about three years before Clare and I met and, to be honest, I was a steaming mess. We wandered into each other's lives and, before we knew it, we were comfortable and set. I never really thought about it until she started making marriage noises. We'd both been married before: she a divorcee with two children as part of the package; me a widower with a void that was sucking in gravity; but it seemed to be the thing to do. I proposed more because it seemed to be what I was supposed to do rather than something I really wanted. But whatever. We got a bigger place together, pooled our resources and, pretty soon, we were the unit you're supposed to be, with two kids and a dog. It seemed to be the thing to do, especially as I didn't have the whole package the first time around. The first time, we'd just run out of time, although we had tried. We tried.

To think I used to be something of a teenage athlete. I'd run cross-country for the school, ploughing on and on, steady and sure, always finishing, always seeing it through, but never quite winning. I was always second or third: respectable performances but never the ones that anyone remembers. But that was when I met Carol.

She was more or less the same age as me and stood at the side of the track with her friends, hanging about after school when the others had gone home. They weren't there for my benefit, though. Carol was the gooseberry for her friend Gemma, a diminutive, round-faced girl who had eyes for one of the other lads. I don't even remember who he was now, but it was the eighties so he had a mullet, an earring and wore his blazer sleeves halfway up his arms as if he was in *Miami Vice*. No mullet for me – my mother cut my hair, and you could tell. Carol and I hit it off though bonding over Tears for Fears and Joy Division. We were teenagers. Music was important. Still is. I don't think the object of Gemma's affections even owned any records, but they had a snog one evening at the end of the playing fields with us all watching, laughing. We all went to get some chips on the way home and Carol decided she and I were going out together. She claimed me and that was that.

To this day, I have no idea what Carol saw in me, especially at that age. We were always so different to each other: me clumsy, she composed; me tactless, she thoughtful; me with wandering hands, she with tightly crossed legs.

The woods remind me of the time when all that changed. Those other woods of my childhood, where the old army fella read his books and warmed his feet by the fire, were so long ago in another time, another world. The last time I went there, the ex-soldier was long gone: we had forgotten about him when we went to secondary school and, by the time Greg and I decided to pay him a return visit, his tent was damp and empty, the books long overtaken by mould and soaked by rain, the last of his possessions trodden into the dirt. We never knew when he had died, and we never would. I looked for any evidence of the old man himself, but there was nothing. It was if he'd soaked into the ground with the rain. I imagined him there, just below the surface, sleeping under the grass.

THE DOG IS PANTING. She lies down with a stick, so I sit on a fallen trunk, mossy and comfortable. I look around. The path seems suddenly unfamiliar; I'm not sure which way we came, and the clearing we're in is denser than I remember. A breeze whispers through the upper branches, but it doesn't stir the air. I wonder if I've imagined it.

The dog looks up at me. 'Shall we go home, girl?' I say. She gets my meaning and stands up. 'Come on then,' I say, and head back in the direction that I think we came from.

The path we take is overgrown, less well-trodden than I remember. We've clearly gone the wrong way, but the woods aren't that big, I reason. I'm sure we'll loop around. It's not like we're in a rainforest with predators around every corner. The path disappears now, so overgrown that I have to kick my way through. It's like I'm just standing in a bush, thorns scratching and catching on my clothes. Give them a couple of months and they'll be sporting blackberries, but right now they're just snagging and dragging. Something skitters and the dog's ears prick up. She dives into the undergrowth and thrashes about vainly. When she emerges, she is on the other side of the mass of brambles. I stamp it down so I can step over to join her.

Another path crosses where we are, seemingly separating two forests. But that can't be. I've been here dozens of times and I've never seen this area. I must be more tired than I thought I was. Last night took more out of me than I had realised. The dog trots over there, investigating new smells, so I follow. It's suddenly cooler somehow, the smell of the trees in the air.

Leaves are on the ground, brown, beige, and brittle. Some have been trodden almost into mulch, soggy with old rainfall. I step around a puddle, slick and muddy. The dog is sniffing the air, and I can sense it too. That word. Petrichor. The smell of the earth after rain. Really, it's not all that unusual for isolated spots to have had rain when the rest of the area is dry. It usually means an isolated cloud is on the move, or I'm walking into or out of it. That's what I tell myself, anyway. It certainly feels unusual enough.

Oak trees rise up around us, the forest floor thick with the crust of fallen autumnal leaves. I really am losing my grip more than usual. I could have sworn it was summer when I left home this morning. Sometimes, the way I remember things doesn't seem to be the way that some other people remember it, so maybe this is another example of me starting to lose it. That's why I like the woods so much: it gives me a respite from distractions, from the worry of not getting it right and the judgement of people.

The oak leaves, interspersed with the shed material of other trees and the plant corpses of the forest floor, form a vast unsolved jigsaw, spreading out beneath the branches. A few feet from the base of the largest oak is something man-made. A makeshift crucifix, made from two twigs no more than an inch each in diameter, tied together with an old shoelace and some blue twine, stands in the ground. Placed at its base, wrapped in a thin plastic bag, the type used to secure leftovers for the freezer, is a framed photograph.

The frame is silver-coated plastic, barely visible through the misty milkiness of the bag. Mould and condensation spots further obscure the details, but a photograph is in the frame. It seems to be an image of a middle-aged couple, the woman with pale skin and shoulders in a dress, and the man slightly taller in a dark suit with something on the lapel. His face is as faint and misty as hers, indistinct through the plastic and condensation.

I bend to pick it up, ignoring the pang in my knee. I hesitate with my hand just an inch away from the wet plastic. I get the feeling suddenly that I shouldn't disturb it, like it's an actual grave or sacred burial site. But it's just a photo wrapped in a sandwich bag. A photo wrapped in a sandwich bag amongst damp autumn leaves in a forest. A forest that was fresh with summer sun just a few minutes ago.

. . .

Carol and I got married earlier than anybody should. We were so young, barely in our twenties, eyes wide open welcoming the life to come that we thought we would experience together. We had no idea really. Registry office, nice reception paid for by her parents, honeymoon somewhere hot with cheap booze and a communal swimming pool, home to a rented flat with a single storage heater. Not before too long, we'd graduated to our first house: a starter box with two bedrooms and nowhere to store the vacuum cleaner. I'd often trip over it on the landing on my way to have a piss in the middle of the night. We meandered along for a few years: I'd trained as a teacher so always had work. Carol lurched from office job to office job, far cleverer and more patient than me, but unlucky with finding something that would stick.

One afternoon, Carol was waiting for me when I got home from work with a splitting plastic bag full of books to mark. She handed me a cup of tea and a teary smile that could only mean one thing. 'I'm pregnant,' she said, simply. I said, 'Holy shit,' but smiled as well. I might even have started crying. We were older than many first-time parents, but younger than we'd planned to be. But we embraced it and she threw herself into choosing prams and cots and all the other paraphernalia that Mothercare had to offer.

After she lost the baby, she was never the same again. Both of us seemed to have left something of ourselves behind in that hospital that night. When she eventually fell ill a few years later, Carol told me with a mixture of equanimity and relief, as if it was what she had expected. The last time we spoke, in a brightly lit room with machines and white sheets, she talked of walking in the woods. In her drugged state, full of pills and comfort, she walked the same path as I did this morning, a child's hand in hers: a child who skipped ahead down the lane, beckoning her to follow.

Today, on the anniversary of Carol's death, I sit on the forest floor, staring at a damp photograph in a plastic bag. I pierce the plastic with my thumbnail and wipe the glass with the back of my hand. Mould has long obscured their features, but the man looks a little overweight, grimacing at the camera as if it's painful for him to stand. The woman – probably his wife – looks a lot like Carol, but I can't see clearly enough. I wipe my eyes and look again. I drop the photo frame in the dirt.

I lie back on the leaves, which feel somehow warm and dry again. The dog snuffles next to me, then her ears suddenly prick up. I hear another dog's bark somewhere along the track: it seems strangely familiar. She looks at me, wagging, as if asking permission to investigate. I wave her off and she bounds through the leaves, barking to the other dog.

Above me is a sky of branches, a net of foliage through which I can see glimpses of sun and cloud. As I close my eyes and my fingers dig into the soil, I forget what brought me here. I breathe the earth, I taste the air, and I take root. I see the whispers of memory in the wood. I hear the blaze of morning in the sun. The forest is with me as my heart slows.

MEDIUM WELL DONE
STEVYN COLGAN

DCI Gavin Quisty was a character that first appeared in the novel *A Murder to Die For*. This short story is one of several that have since been written to expand upon the character.

'THE LOCAL POLICE can't believe that this is a simple suicide. Not if they've bothered to call you in, Quisty.'

William Luckinbill was a short, stocky plum pudding of a man and didn't like drama in his life. Half the reason he'd become a coroner's officer was the fact that dead people tended not to express opinions or make demands on his time.

'But you're hoping that I'll prove them wrong, eh?' Detective Chief Inspector Gavin Quisty smiled and hovered around the body, snapping photographs on his smartphone. 'But it is an odd one and no mistake.'

He brought the phone closer to the victim's face and took several close-ups of the mouth. The horribly smiling mouth.

'Dear lord, that smile is unnerving,' said Luckinbill. 'Something to do with rigor mortis I suppose.'

'Possibly,' said Quisty. 'It's unusual though. What was the time of death?'

'The doctor reckoned about five hours ago, which is about right for rigor to have set in. But usually, once life is extinct, the muscles relax and the face loses all expression. Maybe it's a side effect of the overdose she took? Whatever the reason, it's bloody creepy.'

The deceased was thin, almost skeletal. Quisty knew that she was only in her fifties but her emaciated appearance and wispy white hair made her look a lot older. She lay on top of her bed, dressed in a pair of expensive black silk pyjamas. Her chin, neck and upper torso were sticky and damp with what smelled like orange juice. The bedroom was as tasteful as her nightwear, decorated in creams, blacks and purples with expensive wallpaper and opulent curtains, swags and tails. On the wall opposite the bed hung a cluster of framed photographs of the dead woman when she'd been healthier and laughing, greeting, and hugging a host of famous people. There were actors, politicians, rock stars, even a pope.

'I'll grant you that there is an element of creepiness to this case, especially considering who she is ... was,' said Quisty.

'And, of course, there's that,' said Luckinbill, pointing to the dressing table mirror upon which was written, in lurid cerise lipstick, the stark message: *Got you!* 'But that's not the worst of it. There's the glass too.'

A single glass tumbler stood on the bedside table. Its surface was covered with fine grey powder where it had been dusted for fingerprints. It smelled strongly of orange juice and of something else besides.

'Ah yes the glass. Now that, I will admit, is ... odd,' said Quisty. He peered at the tumbler closely and then began systematically going through the contents of the bedside drawers.

'Odd? It's impossible,' said Luckinbill. 'Someone has made a mistake.'

Quisty's staff officer, DS Kim Woon, appeared at the door.

'I think the girlfriend is up to seeing you now, Guv,' she said. 'She's in the kitchen.'

'Excellent. Then a cup of tea is in order I think.'

As Quisty descended the stairs, he passed by framed posters and magazine covers that reminded him of just how famous the dead woman had once been. It wasn't that long ago when you couldn't turn on a television without seeing Hattie Deverick's smiling face. She had been a hugely popular guest on chat shows and her own TV series *The Other Worlds of Hattie Deverick* had been a fixture of Sunday nights for nearly a decade. As the UK's foremost psychic and medium, she had enjoyed sell-out tours of theatres all over the country and had built up a large and affluent A-List clientele. It was even rumoured that a few of the royals were on her books.

But then it had all come crashing down.

Former stage magician Declan Ivory had made a career out of debunking self-proclaimed psychics. He believed that they preyed on people's grief to earn a living and he pursued them with fervour. In one notable incident he had confronted Deverick's main rival, Jaz Sholto, during a live show which had resulted in an on-stage scuffle and a conviction for assault. But it hadn't deterred him.

Meanwhile, Hattie Deverick remained his prime target and, in 2017, he went public with a searing exposé of her act. Following six years of research and secret filming, he announced that he had discovered the secret of her extraordinary success. Like most self-proclaimed psychics and mediums, he'd said, Deverick was a master of 'cold reading' – a set of techniques that she could use to extract information from another person while always appearing to know much more about the subject than she actually did. However, that was just the tip of the iceberg. Ivory alleged that Deverick and her partner, a dour Welsh Wiccan called Kendra, had developed an exceptionally clever and intricate form of sign language based upon touching parts of the face and upper body. Kendra, who sat in on every public performance, had access to the internet and the ticketing data for the people who had booked to see the show and would signal appropriate answers to her partner on stage when required to do so. As evidence, Ivory produced video footage of Kendra that demonstrated clearly that she was using a tablet and that every movement of her hands, every twitch, every extreme facial expression corresponded exactly to a particular letter or word. And, sure enough, when decoded, her signals always matched the sudden 'revelation' that Deverick would then produce on stage. To add insult to injury, Ivory made his decoding guide freely available and encouraged the public to check for themselves. It became a popular pastime; people began to take a perverse delight in re-watching Deverick's old TV shows while decoding Kendra's subtle but now blatantly obvious signals.

Unsurprisingly, Hattie Deverick's career took a steep nosedive; a fact that delighted her detractors who made great sport of pointing out that 'she hadn't seen that coming'. But worse was to come. Six months after Ivory's revelations, Deverick was diagnosed with breast cancer, something that her more insensitive and boorish critics also pointed out that she hadn't predicted. Near bankruptcy had followed just a few years later; the result of cancelled tours, the loss of her prime-time TV show and expensive private health care bills. When her cancer had gone into remission in 2020 she'd made one last attempt to fight back and regain some of her former glory, but it was all too little too late. Her career was over.

QUISTY ARRIVED in the kitchen and was quietly impressed. It was a beautiful room, large and spacious, and featured a dining area under conservatory glass and a black granite-topped island surrounded by high stools. The walls were covered in dark wood cupboards interspersed with high spec equipment – warming ovens, wine chillers and a massive six burner gas range among them. The kitchen smacked of expensive luxury, as did the rest of the house, which was beautifully appointed if surprisingly modest in size considering how much money the famous psychic must have made in her career. But she had also lost a great deal of money too and downsizing had been unavoidable. That said, she'd still managed to hold on to a substantial four bedroom house on a private road in the nicer part of Tingwell where the neighbours were equally well off and just stuffy and old-fashioned enough to privately disapprove of same sex relationships. Kendra – real name Karen Pantry – hadn't exactly helped matters by declaring herself to be a witch, habitually dressing in black and dancing nude in the back garden to celebrate the eight festivals that annually marked the turning of the 'Wheel of the Year'.

'You must be Kendra,' said Quisty. 'I'm DCI Gavin Quisty and this is DS Kim Woon. I'm so sorry for your loss.'

'Thanks,' said Kendra. She was sitting on a high stool, slumped over the island, a glass of rosé in one hand and tracing something arcane with her black painted fingernail in a small spillage on the counter top. Her voice was empty, emotionless.

'Would you mind if I make us all a tea?' asked Quisty.

'Help yourself,' said Kendra. 'I'm fine with the wine.'

'I'll sort out the tea, Guv,' said Woon. 'At least I will when I figure out where everything is. I've never seen so many cupboards.'

'The teabags are probably near the kettle somewhere,' said Kendra. 'I don't know for sure. Never touch the stuff.'

As Woon began the task of opening cupboards in search of tea, Quisty folded his long body onto a stool.

'I'm afraid that, in cases like this, I am forced to ask you some questions,' he said. 'Do you feel up to it?'

'Sure. You have a job to do. I get that,' said Kendra. 'But I can't tell you any more than I told the other guys earlier. I guess I'm prime suspect, eh?'

'It's more about elimination than accusation,' said Quisty. 'Your fingerprints are on the glass after all.'

'That's because I took her up some orange juice,' said Kendra.

'But I didn't crush up all those tablets and put them in it. And I didn't write that message on the mirror.'

'So you're saying that Miss Deverick did it,' said Quisty.

'No. I'm saying that Ivory did it,' said Kendra.

'By that you mean Declan Ivory the magician?' said Quisty.

'I do.'

'Who died two years ago in a car crash.'

Kendra looked up from her wine. Her heavy black eye make-up was smeared and ran in dark runnels down her cheeks.

'Yeah. He's your murderer,' she growled. 'His fingerprints are on the glass aren't they?'

'You're not actually considering her claims are you?' asked Luckinbill.

'Working with Quisty I've learned never to dismiss anything,' said Woon. She had brought the coroner a cup of tea. Luckinbill had stayed in the victim's bedroom while the forensics officer finished up.

'But you've met her. She's not what I'd call a stable person,' said Luckinbill. 'She thinks that she's a witch and she genuinely believes that she caused Ivory's death by putting a hex on him.'

'Really?' said Woon.

'Really. She says that she put a curse on him and two days later he was dead under the wheels of a 40 ton articulated lorry. Coincidence to be sure but she completely believes that she was responsible,' said Luckinbill. 'As I said, she's unstable. And now she's claiming that the dead man has murdered her girlfriend in revenge.'

'So she says.'

'But even if that were true, which it obviously isn't, why would he do it?' said Luckinbill. 'Ivory spent decades trying to prove that mediums and psychics were frauds, that the afterlife is a fantasy. By murdering someone from beyond the grave wouldn't he be proving that Deverick was right all along?'

'He would be shooting himself in the foot I guess,' said Woon. 'If ghosts can shoot themselves, that is. Or hold a gun. Or have feet.'

'I saw her on stage once at the Majestic in Hoddenford,' said Luckinbill. 'Not really my thing but my mother wanted to go along. She was surprisingly convincing. I mean, I know it was all nonsense but she made it look very real. I enjoyed the show. And Mum was impressed.'

'So were millions of others,' said Woon. 'And you do realise that once word gets out that she's shuffled off this mortal coil, every psychic is going to claim that she has contacted them to affirm that the afterlife is real don't you? Ivory will be spinning in his grave.'

'That's not all he's been doing if the evidence on that glass is to be believed.'

'Yes indeed,' said Woon, tapping her phone against her teeth.

DOWNSTAIRS IN THE KITCHEN, Quisty was leafing through a scrapbook of reviews and press clippings, theatre advertising bills and press photos. Hattie Deverick had been something of a completist, apparently, because she had included just as many bad reviews as good. Towards the back of the book he found a flurry of press clippings about the psychic's infamous final TV appearance.

In 2020, in one last desperate bid to salvage something of her career, Deverick had challenged Declan Ivory to appear with her on a high-profile chat show where, she claimed, she would prove her psychic ability to him, and to the world, once and for all. As an extra inducement, she had insisted that Ivory search her for hidden earpieces or other devices that might be used to trick or deceive. Kendra, meanwhile, would not be allowed anywhere in the studio where she might have line of sight with her partner. Ivory agreed and the show went ahead. To the delight of the show's host, Deverick's abilities appeared to have returned in spades and she scored hit after hit with strangers from the audience. Even Ivory had been impressed, maintaining that it was some form of trick, naturally, but candidly admitting that he couldn't figure out how it was done. Striking while the iron was hot, Deverick had then asked Ivory to perhaps keep an open mind in future and to swear, in front of the audience, that when his time came he might do something for her.

'When you see for yourself that there really is an afterlife, I want you to promise me that you will find some way to make this known to the living,' she'd asked him. 'Then, if the greatest debunker of all time is seen to be sending messages from the afterlife, there can be no more doubt.'

Ivory had readily agreed, sure in his heart of hearts that there was no life after death, and the two adversaries had parted on seemingly good terms, considering their past history.

Just a week later, Ivory was dead.

In the weeks that followed, Hattie Deverick was a celebrity all over again, albeit most often as the partner of the 'self-proclaimed witch who claims that she killed Declan Ivory'. Once again, she, and now Kendra, were appearing on chat shows and magazine programmes. Meanwhile, people all over the world waited eagerly for a sign, any sign to show that Declan Ivory had ascended to a higher plane. Many psychics claimed that he had contacted them but Ivory had anticipated this and had made provisions to dismiss or validate such claims. The day after the TV debate, he had decided upon a certain obscure phrase, written it down and placed it in the safe-keeping of his solicitor. He'd then told the world what he'd done and that, if he were to genuinely make contact from the other side, he would speak the phrase as proof. No one had yet quoted the correct phrase, leading sceptics to affirm what they already knew - that death was simply the end of life. However, the true believers paid this no heed. To them it was obvious that Ivory had either reneged on his deal with Deverick and was being deliberately uncommunicative, or the alleged secret phrase story was all a lie.

Deverick's second taste of fame had been short-lived, however. Just thirteen months after Ivory's death, her cancer had returned more aggressively than ever and her health had quickly deteriorated.

As the second anniversary of her triumphant return to celebrity approached, she had apparently chosen to curtail her life with a glass of orange juice heavily laced with a cocktail of sleeping tablets, painkillers and antidepressants, rather than wait for the terrible disease to run its painful and inevitable course. With her death, one of the most entertaining professional rivalries of recent years had finally come to a tragic end. Or, so it had seemed until the discovery of Declan Ivory's fingerprints on the glass that had taken Deverick's life.

'It's my fault that she's dead,' said Kendra suddenly, breaking Quisty's reverie. 'I don't mean that I poisoned her. I mean because I cursed Ivory and killed him. Among Wiccans, there is a belief that you reap what you sow, that the actions you take – good or bad – will come back to you threefold. It's my fault that her cancer returned and it's my fault that she's dead.'

'You can't blame yourself for her death,' said Quisty. 'There was always a strong possibility that her cancer would return. That's the nature of the disease, sadly.'

'There is a cosmic balance and I tipped it,' said Kendra, miserably. 'The universe is ancient and it doesn't forget. Misfortune will follow me wherever I go from now on. I've already broken a wine glass and a side plate this morning. And I haven't broken anything in years.'

'You've had a terrible shock,' said Quisty. He watched Kendra's trembling hands as she took another sip of wine. 'You're bound to be a little shaky and distracted.'

'You don't understand. Hattie's spirit will be so upset with me,' said Kendra. 'She hated it when things got broken. She was a stickler for having full sets of everything.'

Quisty looked again at the scrapbook, so beautifully organised in chronological order, each section colour coded for theatre work, TV work, books, miscellaneous. A sudden thought struck him.

'Do you mind if I have a look in your kitchen cupboards?' he said.

'Knock yourself out,' said Kendra. 'I guess you think I'm some kind of a nut with all this talk of curses.'

'I've learned never to dismiss anything unless proven to be false beyond all argument,' said Quisty, opening one cupboard and then another. 'And while, I admit, I'm not someone who puts much stock in superstition, I do know that people who fervently believe in things like curses can suffer genuine effects such as anxiety, feelings of helplessness and even heart palpitations and reduced blood pressure. The effects can be real even if the cause is up for debate. I believe that you genuinely believe that your actions in cursing Ivory are the cause of your partner's death.'

'What else am I supposed to believe?' said Kendra. She drained her glass. 'You saw the message written on that mirror. He said, 'Got you!' I killed him and he killed the person I love to make me suffer. He'll be coming for me next.'

'IF YOU ASK ME, the Goth girlfriend did it,' said Luckinbill. 'She had the means; she openly admits that she brought the glass of orange juice up here to the bedroom. And I reckon she forced Miss Deverick to drink it. There's all that spilled juice around her mouth and neck isn't there? That smacks to me of a struggle. She had a good motive too. After all, she'll probably inherit the house and whatever money is still in the bank.'

In the bedroom, the forensics officer had finished up and the undertakers had arrived to collect the deceased. Luckinbill and Woon stood out on the landing and watched the proceedings distractedly.

'But why risk committing murder?' asked Woon. 'Deverick's cancer was very advanced and she can't have had much time left. There's almost nothing left of her. All Kendra had to do was wait a few weeks, a couple of months at worst, and she'd have inherited anyway.'

'Greed makes people impatient. Or maybe she had pressing debts?'

'That still doesn't explain how a dead man's fingerprints came to be on the glass though does it?' said Woon.

'No,' admitted Luckinbill. 'I can't begin to explain that.'

'I'm going to pop back down to the kitchen and see how the boss is getting on,' said Woon.

'No problem. We're pretty much done up here now,' said Luckinbill.

WOON FOUND Quisty sitting in the sunlit dining area and watching a video on his smartphone.

'Have you ever seen this, Kim?' he asked. 'It's Hattie Deverick's last television appearance, that final showdown she had with Declan Ivory on that BBC chat show.'

On the screen, Deverick could be seen with a smug smile on her face, while Ivory nervously drank from a glass of water. He looked rattled.

'I saw it at the time,' said Woon. 'She ran rings around him.'

'I wonder how she did it?'

'You mean you haven't figured that out yet?' teased Woon. 'You're losing your touch.'

'Give me a little more time, Kim,' said Quisty. 'But I think we can be pretty sure that it wasn't due to any psychic powers.'

'With all due respect, we have more pressing matters to worry about,' said Woon.

'You mean her death?' said Quisty. 'Oh, I know how that happened.'

'What?'

'The answer is in the cupboards,' said Quisty.

'What do you mean 'The answer is in the cupboards'?'

'Tell me. Have you ever played that memory game when you put a bunch of items on a tea tray and ask someone to memorise what's there?' asked Quisty. 'Then you remove one object while they're not looking and they have to try to remember what the object was?'

'Sure. Lots of times when I was a kid,' said Woon.

'I was always devilishly good at it,' said Quisty. 'From quite an early age I realised that I have a near eidetic memory. It's proven to be very useful at crime scenes. And today it has been invaluable.'

'Did something change at the crime scene then?' asked Woon. 'If it did, I missed it.'

'No it didn't,' said Quisty. 'But I see things and I remember where I've seen them and then …'

'You find connections between them.'

'Exactly,' said Quisty. 'It's always about the connections. I've seen today, for example, a glass bearing the fingerprints of a man dead for two years. I've seen a grinning corpse. I've seen a message written in lipstick on a mirror. And I've seen that Miss Deverick had something amounting to obsessive compulsive behaviour. Her girlfriend told me that if any of the china got broken, she would have a hissy fit and the item would have to be replaced as soon as possible to keep the set complete.'

'That's not particularly OCD,' said Woon. 'My Mum would probably do the same.'

'Yes indeed,' said Quisty. 'But I'd wager that your mother also has a few random items in her kitchen. Perhaps a 'World's Greatest Mum' mug you bought for her birthday? Or a classic 'Brown Betty' teapot that doesn't match any other piece of crockery. A comedy eggcup. A single rogue spoon. Almost everyone does. But not Miss Deverick. All of the saucepans match. Her cooking utensils all have the same handles. And her place settings are similarly uniform: twelve dinner plates, twelve bowls, twelve wine glasses, twelve sets of cutlery. Twelve of everything and all matching. No deviant items at all to be found.'

'Okay, so maybe she was a bit obsessive,' said Woon. 'But what has that got to do with all of the other stuff you mentioned?'

'Think, Kim, think!' said Quisty. 'How many glass tumblers should there be in this kitchen?'

'From what you've said, I assume twelve.'

'Exactly!' said Quisty.

. . .

'And you're absolutely sure that it's a case of suicide?' said Luckinbill.

'One hundred per cent positive,' said Quisty.

'Thank goodness for that,' said Luckinbill. 'The last thing we need around here is a murder. This is sleepy leafyville. We don't have murders in Hoddenford. We have angina and gout and death by over-exertion while pulling leeks on the allotment. And no ghosts either I take it?'

'Not even a wisp of ectoplasm,' said Quisty. 'This was all about revenge.'

'She committed suicide to get revenge? On who?'

'Declan Ivory of course,' said Quisty. 'The man who destroyed her career. This was Hattie Deverick's final gift to her many admirers and colleagues - proof that the afterlife exists and that Declan Ivory was wrong, all in one deliciously malicious act of *felo de se*.'

'But what about the fingerprints on the glass?' said Luckinbill. 'And the message on the mirror?'

'Oh, they really are Declan Ivory's prints,' said Quisty. 'Perhaps you'd tell Mr Luckinbill how they got there, Kendra?'

Kendra's eyes dropped to the floor.

'I don't know what you mean.'

'It's a water glass from the TV studio where your partner made her last appearance,' said Quisty. 'I can show you the glass on this video of the show if you like.'

He held up his phone.

Kendra sighed deeply and fat tears ran down her cheeks.

'He was such a cocky bastard. I just wanted to teach him a lesson,' she said. 'I didn't mean to kill him.'

'So, after everyone left the set, you swiped Ivory's glass, didn't you? You knew that it would carry his fingerprints and some of his DNA. And you were going to use that to place a curse on him for what he'd done to the woman you love, yes?'

'Yes! The glass was my poppet, my talisman. I used it to cast the spell that killed him.'

'No, you didn't,' said Quisty. 'What killed him was a tired Croatian long-haul lorry driver called Roko who fell asleep at the wheel. So what did you do with the glass after you'd used it?'

'I sealed it up in a jiffy bag and hid it in one of the lesser used kitchen cupboards; somewhere dark, like you're supposed to,' said Kendra. 'Of course, when Ivory actually died I had to tell Hattie what I had done. She wasn't happy.'

'I thought she hated him?' said Woon.

'She did,' said Kendra. 'But she hadn't wanted him dead. Of course, I couldn't cancel the curse or lift it because the damage had been done. So I just tried to forget it.'

'But Miss Deverick didn't forget did she?' said Quisty. 'She was in constant pain and so, she thought, why not kill two birds with one stone – herself and Ivory's credibility?'

'Ah I see,' said Woon. 'So she used the glass that Kendra pocketed to administer the drugs to herself.'

'She knew that Ivory had a criminal record for assault and that his fingerprints would be on file. She also knew that we'd fingerprint the glass as a matter of course,' said Quisty. 'Which would reveal the most extraordinary evidence of Ivory taking action from beyond the grave.' 'But wait ... I took her the orange juice,' said Kendra. 'And I used one of the tumblers from the kitchen.'

'Yes you did,' said Quisty. 'And I found that same tumbler in Miss Deverick's bedside drawers among ... other things. My guess is that she transferred the juice from the glass you brought up to the glass with Ivory's prints on it, spilling a fair amount on herself while doing so.'

'I don't understand any of this,' said Kendra.

'I knew that the suicide glass had a story to tell when I saw that it was a different design from the one hidden in the drawer and the eleven others I found in the kitchen cupboards,' explained Quisty. 'And why would a person so intent on keeping rigidly to twelve place settings hang on to a thirteenth glass? It had to have some kind of special significance. And then I watched the video of the TV show and saw Ivory drinking from an identical glass to the one on the bedside table. The clincher was taking another look at the glass and seeing that it was marked as 'Property of the BBC' on the base.'

'So if Ivory didn't kill her, who wrote the message on the mirror?' asked Kendra. 'Because it certainly wasn't me.'

'It was written by Miss Deverick,' said Quisty. 'We read it as Ivory saying 'Got you!' to her when, in fact, it was Miss Deverick saying 'Got you!' to him.'

'Oh my god,' said Kendra.

'One last brilliant performance,' said Quisty. 'Freedom from pain, freedom from shame, freedom from money worries and a final snook magnificently cocked at Declan Ivory.'

'Amazing,' said Luckinbill. 'No wonder she died smiling.'

'You know I hate loose ends, don't you?' said Woon as she drove Quisty back towards Uttercombe and home.

'I do,' said Quisty. 'Mildly obsessive even.'

'No, just tidy and organised,' said Woon. 'And it's bugging me that, after all that we uncovered today, the one thing we didn't find out was how Hattie Deverick managed to fool Ivory and everyone else during that last TV appearance. I've watched the video over and over again. Am I missing something? She didn't have any real psychic powers, did she?'

'No. No psychic powers. Just Bluetooth,' said Quisty.

'Explain,' said Woon.

'It wasn't just a glass that I found in those bedside drawers,' said Quisty. 'Without going into prurient detail, I can say that our lady medium was in possession of a number of ... toys.'

'Oh! You mean ...'

'Yes I do. And I couldn't help noticing that one of them was small, like an egg, and had a wireless remote control which, presumably, can be operated by the user or by someone they trust,' said Quisty.

'Oh,' said Woon.

'Well, quite. And it got me thinking. I'm pretty sure that Ivory's search of Miss Kendrick for technological aids did not involve an ... intimate element. And I know that, while Kendra wasn't allowed to be in line of sight with her partner during the TV interview, she was allowed backstage. Certainly within the range for Bluetooth devices anyway.'

'So you think that Deverick went on stage with one half of the device in ... er ... on her person, and Kendra sent her messages using the remote?'

'I do,' said Quisty. 'If you watch the video carefully there is, more often than not, a little quiver of ... something across Miss Deverick's face before she answers each question. By the end of the show she was positively glowing.'

'Bloody hell,' said Woon. 'So you reckon they used Morse code maybe? Buzzz Buzz Buuuuzzzz Buzz.'

'Or a code of their own devising,' said Quisty. 'They were good at that sort of thing after all. I don't suppose that Kendra will ever admit to it though.'

Woon smiled.

'Puts a whole new spin on the phrase 'internal dialogue'.'

The Last Appointment
Virginia Moffatt

T he Minister for War entered the safe room, switching on the light to disperse the shadows. Outside, the heavily fortified bunker, the last remnant of the winter sun seeped through the purple clouds, a blood-red wound in a bruised sky. Darkness was coming and very soon. He should have left hours ago, but his last appointment – the most important of the day – was running late.

The building was nearly empty. Apart from a skeleton security team downstairs and the gunners above, there was only him left. Once his visitor was gone, they would depart together, and the building, where he had worked for so many years, would be abandoned. But for now, it was time to Zoom his wife to inform her of the delay. There was one computer in the room; chosen because of its secure wifi. He turned it on, started the meeting and waited for her to sign in. Her voice arrived first, a disembodied ghost echoing from behind her photograph before she switched the camera on, revealing a pale, round-faced brunette. Another person might have noticed the lines on her skin, the purple shadows under her eyes, the tension in her posture. But the Minister was a busy man, not an observant one; the lines and shadows passed him by.

'You're still there?'

'I'm waiting for my last appointment.'
'You should have rescheduled.'
'This meeting is too important.'
'It always is.' Even he couldn't miss the weary sarcasm in her voice.
'It really is a matter of life and death.'
'If you say so.' She looked over her shoulder, startled by a noise behind her.
'What was that?'
'Just a door banging. It's windy up here...' She turned back again, this time in response to a child's voice, "That's Jessie. Must go. Come soon. We miss you.'
'I'll be with you soon. I promise.' She put her hand to the screen as she signed off, where it remained frozen in a permanent farewell. A more sentimental man might have touched the screen as a gesture of the importance of their relationship. But the Minister was as unsentimental as he was unobservant. He didn't give the hand, or his wife, another thought. Switching off the computer he left the room for the last time.

He walked along the corridor, turning at the end to join the long passage that ran the front of the building. A decade ago, he could look out from these windows over the most glorious of cities. How often had he stood here at just this time, watching as the white walls of the Winter Palace turned slowly pink? As the windows of the iconic Triangle Tower blazed in the red rays of the setting sun? And the wide streets, grand houses and parks were lit up with a warm orange glow, so that even the grim high rises and shanty town beyond were momentarily beautiful?

They were gone now, all gone. Ten years of endless bombing had reduced the city to a wasteland of rubble and ash. The Winter Palace was razed to the ground in the early bombardments, causing the Royal Family to flee to the safety of the north. All that remained of the Tower were the rusting steel girders rising out of shards of broken glass. The previously populous streets were now empty, the houses reduced to dust, the parks full of burnt-out trees. The river, once home to catfish, eels, avocets and warblers, was now a black morass, silted up with debris from explosions and oil leaked from the refinery accident a few months earlier. No fish or fowl could survive in it now; they had long since departed. As had those citizens lucky enough to escape in the time before the sieges, when the migration routes were relatively easy and plentiful. Not everyone got away of course, those less healthy or wealthy remained, eking out an existence, hiding in basements from the worst of the bombs, reliant on local militia for food, water and safety. But the vast majority had gone, never to return. And after this appointment, he would finally follow them, taking the helicopter home to his family before flying north to safety and freedom.

The last ray of sun dipped below the smoke-filled horizon. In the distance, he could see flashes of mortar and hear the sound of gunfire, closer than he'd anticipated. He switched the button to close the blackout blinds, continuing down the corridor as they slid down the windows, blocking out the world. The green emergency lights flickered on, illuminating the portraits of men who had once led armies from this building. The older paintings depicted generals with plumed hats and medalled chests, astride large horses, swords dangling down their sides. More recently the uniforms had turned to khaki, and then, as civil servants had gained ascendance, the subjects dressed in sombre grey suits. He glanced at them nervously. He used to feel confident they would approve of the job he had done to save his nation, but the rapid advance of the enemy in recent days was making him less sure of himself. Today he couldn't help feeling their eyes were gazing down on him in judgement.

He turned the corner, trying to shake off such unhelpful thoughts, and then frowned at the chink of light coming out of his room; he could have sworn he had left the light off. He stiffened, scanning about him for signs of danger. There were none. Even so, he tiptoed towards it, hardly daring to breathe, until he arrived at the doorway and saw a figure sitting in his favourite leather armchair.

'You don't mind, do you?' A familiar, lean face smiled up at him. 'Only I was early, and the guard said I could come up.'

'Not at all,' the Minister returned his smile as casually as he could. It would not do to indicate how relieved he felt, even with an ally as old as this. 'Drink?' The other man raised a glass of whisky, 'I thought, since it was our last time in this building, you wouldn't object.'

'No,' again, though his visitor's casual assumption was annoying, it wouldn't do to show any irritation. As usual, they had business to do, and it was in both their interests to conduct it as swiftly as possible. He walked over to the cabinet, poured himself a single malt and sat down. The guns were louder now, louder than they should be. The invaders were closer than predicted; he didn't like it.

'I do like this room,' his visitor said, glancing at the large oak table, the King's portrait, the flag adorning the wall. 'I always enjoy working amidst the trappings of the State. Particularly when you think how we began.'

He nodded, all those years in secret meetings, in far-flung places, in the days when they were both deniable. They were young then and totally reckless, drinking in the face of each oncoming storm, always staying till the last moment it was safe to do so. He realised with a lurch in his stomach that this long conflict had dampened his appetite for such excitements, particularly with the gunfire so close.

'That was another life.'

'True...entertaining though it was at the time, I think I prefer being your government's Saviour,' his companion smiled.

'And I, my current status,' nodded the Minister. 'This war has been good for us.'

'Indeed it has.' His companion drained the last of the whisky.

A bomb exploded half a mile away, and as enemy planes screeched overhead, it was time to finish their business so they could make their escapes.

'Speaking of which, I hope you have the confirmations required?'

'Indeed I do.' His guest leant forward, opening his locked briefcase with his skeletal hands.

'And a secure connection?' This transaction was too sensitive even for the Ministry's wifi – his companion's system was less likely to be hacked.

'Of course.' The guest pulled out a computer, placing it on his lap, his long, white fingers tapping on the keyboard. 'Part 1.' He handed the screen over to the Minister who scanned the documents – the inventories and code words matched.

'And Part 2?'

'In this envelope, sealed by myself at the border.'

The Minister took it, opened the seal and smiled. The location for the handover was perfect. A disused quarry five miles from the Army's Field Headquarters, protected on all sides by high mountains. He picked up his phone, dialled a number and sent the coordinates through. 'A unit will be dispatched immediately to protect the convoy and guide it home.'

'And payment?'

'On confirmation of a safe rendezvous, as usual. Another drink?' His companion nodded. It was unusual for the Minister to celebrate before completion, but this was an unusual day. Once the unit arrived, there would be enough weaponry to turn the war in their favour again. Within six months, they could liberate the capital, the enemy would be forced into retreat, the government could return and his place in history would be assured.

The men sat in companionable silence, waiting for the phone to ring. They were not exactly friends, but their mutual experiences made them closer than most business acquaintances. And it meant that, as the bombs fell ever closer, it was comforting to be sitting together waiting for the call.

The Minister glanced at his watch. Shouldn't be too long now. Another bomb exploded and then in the distance, an impossible sound. That couldn't be the rumble of tanks? They were supposed to be a day away. All the intelligence reports had said so. The phone ringing was a distraction from the nagging anxiety that he might have left it too late, and the voice at the other end was smoothly reassuring. He smiled as he hung up, sending the email immediately.

'Transfer going through now.'

'Received, with thanks.' His guest stood up and they shook hands. 'Pleasure doing business with you.'

'Always.'

'And now if you don't mind, I think it is time we both...' He didn't finish his sentence. A huge blast knocked them both to the floor. It was followed by a muffled explosion that sounded even closer, and more worrying still, the unmistakable rumble of tanks.

'Oh dear,' said his visitor, as he picked his cadaverous limbs up off the floor.

'We need to leave, immediately.'

'It is too late for that I am afraid.'

'What do you mean?'

'Your capital is lost. In the next half an hour troops will be storming this building.'

'Impossible. They are too far away.'

'You are quite wrong about that, I'm afraid.'

'But the intelligence reports...'

'You are forgetting the enemy within.'

'Sorry?'

'All those families whose sons you locked up, whose daughters you enslaved, did it never occur to you that one day they might turn against you? That when another leader marched through the country promising justice and freedom, they might be tempted to try something new?'

'All the more reason, to go, now.'

The Minister couldn't understand why his guest was hesitating. He was usually the first to escape in times of trouble. A second explosion rocked the front of the building and voices shouted in triumph. It wasn't safe to stay here. He made for the door.

'As I told you, it is too late, my friend.'

He felt a strong arm on his shoulder as he was guided back to the chair, 'Your army is defeated. Look.'

The Minister gazed in disbelief at the images on the other man's phone. The airfield in flames, an enemy flag fluttering above the body of the General face first on the ground. And worst still, hundreds of government troops embraced their conquerors.

'What...? How?'

'One man's invasion is another's liberation it would seem.'

'But the weapons?'

'In the hands of your enemies very shortly I expect.'

'You knew... you took our money and you knew...' The Minister stared at his guest.

'Why so surprised? It's not the first time, after all. Though I do regret that it is the first time with you.'

'I don't understand.'

The other man smiled a grim smile. 'I've always been honest about this. You know I sell to the highest bidder. That used to be your government. Today, I'm afraid, that is no longer the case.'

'We must leave.'

'That option is no longer available. Your helicopter has been destroyed. You have no way out.'

'You must have a plan, you always do. Take me with you.'

'Naturally, I do. But... you know why I can't do that. Once, perhaps, I'd have risked it, but now, I'm afraid, you are too much of a liability.'

The Minister stared at him, 'We've known each other for years.'

'And because I respect that relationship, I'm offering you an escape,' he reached in his briefcase and took out a small pill and put it on the table. 'Believe me, this will be quick and painless, which we both know will be much better than the alternative. And, for the record, I truly am sorry it has ended this way.'

He packed his things away, locking his case with a sharp click as another explosion rocked the building. The Minister stared at the pill in disbelief.

'Your choice of course, Minister, but I really wouldn't leave it too long to decide.'

The Minister took the pill, holding it in his hand for a moment, how could his life be reduced to this? How could he be even contemplating it? He had a wife, a child. How could it be that he would never see them again? His visitor had to be wrong. He was about to throw it away when the floor shook again with the sound of a bomb exploding near the front entrance, it wouldn't be long till it was breached. He shuddered remembering the ransacking of a regional ministry a few months ago. The men and women dragged out of the building and hacked to death on the street, the rest locked in the building which the army burned to the ground. He picked the pill up, placing it on his tongue.

'Quick and painless you say?'

'Of course.'

He closed his eyes, trying to picture his wife, his child, but all he could see was a horde of people running towards him ready to take his life.

'Goodbye then,' he swallowed the tablet in one gulp.

'Goodbye.'

His guest watched as the pill did its work. It was as pain-free and swift as he'd promised. He closed the Minister's eyes and left the room five minutes before the crowds broke through the front entrance.

He ran through the building taking the backstairs to a small entrance where an armoured car and team of bodyguards was waiting for him. As they raced through streets filled with smoke and fire, he checked his bank balance. A second payment, double that of the first, had just been transferred, confirming the wisdom of switching sides. He thought of the Minister and sighed. It was regrettable that he could not be saved, but there was no point brooding about it. The time was better spent preparing for his next deal.

The car sped on through the ruined suburbs, out past the smaller towns that had seen little fighting and away into the open countryside. Technically they were safe now, all the intelligence reports suggested the remaining government troops were stationed over in the west, but he knew better than most how unreliable intelligence could be. So, he remained alert to every strange sound, or odd light in the sky, as they hurried through the darkness to the border.

Thankfully, the night passed uneventfully. As the watery sun rose above the misty forests, they at last crossed into safety, soon stopping at a small roadside café to enjoy a generous breakfast. He allowed himself a small sigh of relief. Tonight, they would take a break at a local hotel and tomorrow he would make his way to the capital for his next appointment with yet another minister of yet another government only too eager to do business with him. He sighed. This country was beautiful, it would be nice, perhaps to rest and holiday here, walk in the hills, swim in the lakes.

But alas! there was never any rest for the wicked. And, with so many countries fighting for land and freedom, always, always, another deal to be done.

SNUFFR

OR HOW BRITAIN BECAME A NICER PLACE

PAUL WATERS

What made the new *Snuffr* app so popular so quickly was that it democratised killing. It brought the ability to snuff out those persistently annoying people who plague us all, within reach of us all. Safe, clean and free. We learned later that everything has a cost.

Henry Tweasle downloaded the app onto his smartphone after Christmas. He used the iTunes voucher he'd been given – the classic gift for the relative for whom you can't be bothered to find something personal. Intriguing adverts for *Snuffr* had been popping up on his social media. *'It could be you! (So make it them instead.)'*

Henry felt got at every day. Got at, intimidated, disrespected and powerless. He'd tried glaring. Didn't help. Often made things worse.

Henry hated the bloke who parked his van outside his house. But what could he do? Henry tried not to show his humiliation when he had to walk around youths blocking the pavement.

Next door's music was so loud he dare not open his windows. Not to mention the language. It was intolerable. But he did tolerate it. He had to. The man from the council had said so. In writing.

According to Mr Arsenne Tunk, Head of Neighbourliness and Social Cohesion, Henry's complaints were insignificant, undocumented hearsay. The council had no resources to send round a noise abatement officer. There were no grounds to rehouse Henry. And no, they couldn't guarantee to preserve his anonymity if he persisted with these frivolous accusations which, frankly, verged on harassment.

Henry sat and seethed as the *Snuffr* app installed. He clicked on the lion's face icon and *Snuffr* opened on his phone...

Like most people, Henry had only heard of *Snuffr* after the huge row over the criminal justice system. The Progressive Alliance coalition government had made direct democracy the core of its uneasy association, so parliament seemed less remote from the people. That meant referenda.

Everyone agreed that the police and courts couldn't deal with chronic antisocial behaviour and the sort of offence that caused outrage – like dodgy banking – but wasn't quite a criminal offence. Various options were mooted, including vigilante groups. They were spun as a return to the traditional values of Henry VIII, but the knee-capping provision for repeat offenders was undermined when the feasibility study was revealed to have been carried out by former IRA members. It was dropped entirely when irate callers to Radio 4's *Any Answers* complained that local vigilantes would create a post code lottery with inconsistent penalties across the country.

Eventually, as part of the political deal permitting Scotland to break away, the coalition amended the death penalty bill. It was mainly aimed at those convicted of murdering immigration guards. But the bill also allowed punishment for low-level nuisance to be subcontracted out for a trial period.

No one was surprised when *Seeco Entertainment*, immediately nicknamed *Psycho,* won the contract. As with the company's once-popular television talent show, applicants queued to nominate, though this time not themselves, but joy riders, love cheats, office sexists, those guys who never buy a round and other undesirables. Each week on *You Choose*, the public voted on who should get the chop.

Those miscreants gaining the most votes were to be discreetly put to sleep and their organs redistributed to deserving recipients – injured soldiers, poorly midwives and celebrities whose livers had taken a battering over their years of charity work.

However, the scheme derailed when *Psycho* founder Timon Bowell immediately topped the charts. So amidst government spin that *You Choose* had been hacked by North Korea, the programme was suspended "pending further refinement".

It never returned. But the seeds had been planted.

So when adverts for *Snuffr* appeared on Henry's social media, he – like most people – was not entirely sure of the legalities. It seemed a grey area. Like ordering cheap Viagra online – not exactly criminal, but not something you'd shout about either – even if it was making the world a happier place.

The "About Us" section of the app explained that the lion's face symbol was derived from the *bocche di leoni* – the lion's mouth carvings in the Doge's Palace in 14th century Venice. The mouth was a letter-box into which people could post denunciations of wrongdoers. *Snuffr* offered a streamlined modern route to retribution.

All Henry needed to do was to submit a link to his target's social media page and the app would do the rest. It promised that the target would be removed within a reasonable period of time, for no fee beyond the original app download price, as long as Snuffr was given access to Henry's email contacts and friends on social media – a minimum of 1,000 names. That must be how it's spreading so fast, thought Henry.

Otherwise, the small print was refreshingly short. It reminded users that the app was only to be used by victims against those responsible, and not for commercial gain, spite, racism, sexism, homophobia or sectarianism. 'If you're using this for the wrong reasons, WE WILL KNOW!'

Grievances had to be current, not historical. Henry presumed that was so *Snuffr* staff could check out the behaviour of targets before carrying out the job. Otherwise it would be open season on every remaining children's TV presenter and DJ.

But who to target? The next scam caller to ask me if I've been in a car accident is in grave danger, thought Henry. *Snuffr* made it seem so easy. Like being a drone pilot. Press a button and whoosh – someone somewhere gets it. No fuss. No mess. Not at this end anyway.

Henry wasn't sure how the other end *did* work. No one really was. But he'd never heard of any complaints. It was a *Which?* best buy.

A rattling outside distracted him. He pushed aside the curtain slightly. Number 33 was putting out her wheelie bin. A day early. What was the point of rules if people ignored them? He glared at her. He saw her pause and look his way. She can't possibly see me, he told himself. Just stay still. Being caught curtain twitching was vaguely shaming. Not that I've anything to be ashamed of, Henry reminded himself.

He sat back down. Could he really go through with it? Might as well, he thought. I've already paid to download it.

Snuffr didn't fund itself solely by downloads. It ran a popular online channel showing its own *Snuffr Movies* – footage of killings where there had been a breach of the terms and conditions. The videos helped the police build criminal cases against rogue *Snuffr* users.

Each movie was prefaced with a copy of the user's declaration that they had freely entered into a conspiracy to kill the target. Damning evidence. But *Snuffr* promised users that their formal admissions of conspiracy would never be made public – except in the event of a breach of the Ts&Cs.

The app also brought in serious money in sponsorship. Both the *Wow Factor* and *The Strictly British Celebrity Love Tank* paid to associate their brands with *Snuffr* – with the added benefit that their judges and presenters gained immunity from being targeted. The BBC was still refusing to cooperate. Everyone agreed that a certain judge had stepped down from *Strictly* just in time.

The only drawback was that you could only get rid of one person each. Henry consulted his mental list. Impossible to whittle it down with so many arseholes in his neighbourhood, never mind the world. If he could just escape and start again. He picked up the letter from the council. Nope. No chance. Mr Tunk had been unequivocal. Henry was stuck.

Unless...

Bit of an unusual surname that, thought Henry. He typed Tunk into his Facebook search. Not many. Add in the first name. Bingo. Even gives his job title in his profile, as if he's actually proud of it.

Henry copied and pasted the link to Mr Arsenne Tunk's personal Facebook page into *Snuffr*.

He sits behind his desk like a god, playing with people's lives, thought Henry. Time he knew what that feels like.

He pressed send. The lion's mouth opened wide and roared.

Henry's immediate feeling of empowerment soon passed, and he entered an uneasy limbo. He felt different, but nothing seemed to change.

Days passed. Weeks. Then another envelope from the council arrived. His heart sank. It was from the Neighbourliness and Social Cohesion Unit. Henry braced himself for the latest bad news from Mr Tunk.

But it wasn't from Mr Tunk. A new member of staff apologised for the delay in dealing with his case. Would Henry Tweasle be available to discuss his rehousing request at his earliest convenience?

Henry felt breathless. He sat down. Stunned. He'd never felt like this before. He read the letter again. It was real. He clenched his fists and allowed himself to believe. Yes!

But what about Mr Tunk? Henry looked him up again on Facebook. His timeline was full of tributes and condolences. Henry was surprised. Apparently Tunk had friends. Henry felt a momentary qualm. Then he shrugged, they were only Facebook friends. And the world was definitely better without Arsenne Tunk. Henry's life was anyway.

His smartphone buzzed twice. Messages. Henry didn't get many, so he opened them at once. They were both from *Snuffr*. The first was a brief questionnaire: 'How was our service?' Henry gave them five out of five. The second message was more puzzling.

Apparently *Snuffr* was having difficulty accessing Henry's list of 1,000 email contacts and social media friends as per the terms and conditions. He frowned. But I don't have 1,000 friends on Facebook or anywhere else. Nowhere near that. I wouldn't want to.

He read on. 'Please confirm that you have at least 1,000 different friends or connections on social media: YES or NO.' Henry clicked NO.

A new screen appeared. 'Dear *Snuffr* user, as per our contract, in exchange for successful completion of your application, you agreed to supply a minimum number of contacts. Your failure to do so breaches our terms and conditions.'

Henry froze. Then read on.

'You now have two options.

- 1. Do nothing. *Snuffr* will release your information to the police and *Snuffr*'s online *Snuffr Movies* channel.
- 2. Successfully carry out a removal service for *Snuffr*. This will wipe clear your breach of contract and also entitle you to a bonus credit to one further use of *Snuffr*. (Failure to complete will lead to automatic activation of option 1.)

Please select your preferred choice.'

Henry's jaw dropped. He checked the terms and conditions. 1,000 names. He had read it but not paid much attention. No one took online friends seriously surely. Except the *Snuffr* marketing department, he realised.

And it was too late to go back. The deed was done. Option 1 would send him straight to jail. He knew he'd never survive there, locked up with murderers.

He read Option 2 again. The language was polite, but there was no doubt what it meant.

I could never kill anyone, thought Henry, could I? I'm too weak. Too scared. I can't fire a gun or strangle someone. It's ridiculous.

But I can't go to jail.

His phone buzzed. Another message from *Snuffr*. 'If no choice is indicated, Option 1 will be registered automatically on your behalf.' Henry saw a stopwatch on-screen counting down from three minutes to zero.

Wait, he thought. I need time to think. I can't kill anyone. I can't go to jail. I don't know any killers. Henry grasped at that thought. *Snuffr* must protect people like him. It wouldn't make sense otherwise. If he hadn't broken the rules this would never have happened. If he followed the rules exactly in future, *Snuffr* would make it alright. That's what they promised.

Ten seconds to go.

He selected Option 2. The countdown stopped. He breathed out. A stay of execution. For him. He understood it meant the end for someone else.

But Henry refused to feel guilty. He had put up with so much for so long. And now things were finally beginning to go right. He deserved a new start. He'd earned it.

Yes, it would all work out. *Snuffr* must have to deal with people like him all the time. Genuine victims. It wouldn't give him a target he couldn't handle. It would probably be someone elderly, on their own. Someone who wouldn't be missed. Like himself, he admitted. *Snuffr* surely appreciated that its users weren't all James Bond types.

His phone buzzed again. *Snuffr*'s lion face appeared with a new message: 'Your target has been selected by *Snuffr* users. We have assessed that the world will be better for their removal. Please scroll down for target information.'

Henry's mouth was dry. He needed a cuppa. Then he noticed a new digital stopwatch. This time the countdown was from seven days. Four minutes were gone already.

Better get on with it, he thought. Get it out of the way.

He had always felt secretly superior to everyone else. Being selected like this confirmed it. Whoever it is must deserve it, he rationalised. They always do.

He scrolled down and scanned the details.

It was as he'd expected. Typical loser. Keeps himself to himself. The neighbours probably suspect he's a paedophile. No loss. Let's have a look at him.

Henry's stomach twisted. He fought down the urge to vomit. He saw himself looking back out from the screen.

And beside his face, the time counting down.

Henry sat very still for a long moment.

Better get on with it, he thought. Get it out of the way.

He went to the shed for some rope.

Like all fads, *Snuffr* eventually faded. The police became alarmed at losing their official monopoly of violence as neighbourhood disputes escalated into deadly vendettas.

The government ordered water companies to quietly add cannabinoids and ecstasy to the supply. The dental lobby got fluoride slipped into the cocktail. The result was that the population of England and Wales became significantly mellower and more tolerant. Short-term memory loss from the ecstasy helped. Their smiles were better too, thanks to the fluoride.

People became nicer. Permanently.

These days, historians say *Snuffr* undermined the fighting spirit that once made Britain great. But the British have become the new darlings of the world. A British passport prompts welcoming smiles wherever we go. From Shanghai to Sao Paulo, people know we love to party and that there's never any trouble.

Seize your freedom with both hands
A.B. Kyazze

Seize your freedom with both hands. Nadia stared at the message on the woman's t-shirt as she walked towards her on the crowded pavement. The woman's face, hiding behind large tortoiseshell sunglasses, revealed nothing. The pink-and-green camouflage fabric stretched close across her chest. The letters were painted-on, glittery-silver and moved slightly with her steps. Nadia couldn't resist the urge to turn and look at the woman again after she had passed. The shirt continued the camouflage, but no words. Her jeans were tight and emphasized one bum cheek at a time.

What does that mean, 'seize your freedom'? Nadia puzzled over it. What if you hadn't figured out how to do that? What if you weren't sure you were the type of person to seize anything?

The woman walked with such confidence. No hurry – people would be waiting for her to arrive. No stress – a woman of her caliber, with her sense of self-worth, wouldn't take shit from anyone.

Nada closed her eyes for a moment and tried to walk like her. To feel like her. To *be* like her. That was what she needed. To be that confident.

'Look out!' a guy shouted. Nadia opened her eyes to see she was walking straight into a dog's lead as it was crouching on the pavement. The dog, a small, overly-anxious white ball, looked at Nadia with big eyes as it strained to make its mound. Nadia tripped a little as she jumped to the side. The guy holding the lead shook his head and then looked back down at his phone. No apology. No plastic bag to hand. He clearly had no intention of stooping down to do the right thing.

At least she didn't step in it. Nadia hurried her pace to get back to the office. She was under pressure to cut her lunch hour short because her boss was going on vacation for two weeks, barking out orders like there was no tomorrow. He knew who he was, the man in charge, and could demand anything.

'You shouldn't let him get away with that, you know,' Shelia insisted on continuing the conversation, even though Nadia was in the toilet cubicle. Sheila was already at the basins, washing her hands and then applying her after-lunch lipstick.

"What'd I do? I just don't know what I did to piss him off so badly." Nadia flushed and opened the door.

'You didn't do anything. It's written all over your face: *doormat.*'

'Shut up! It's not.'

Sheila smacked her lips. She prided herself on telling it like it is. 'You need to stand up for yourself. Otherwise bosses like him will always walk all over you.'

'Sorry, you're right. I know you're right.'

'And don't say sorry all the time. It's the same thing.'

'Right, sorry, I mean... oh, just forget it.'

Nadia's boss whirled his way out of the office, passport, boarding pass and last-minute print-outs all in his briefcase. He was still yelling out demands as the revolving door swooshed away the sound of his voice.

Nadia went back to her desk, and Googled 'Seize Your Freedom' and 'pink camouflage.' Turned out that H&M sold the shirt, quite cheap. She bought two, as she wasn't sure of her size.

'HE'S BACK,' Sheila hissed. Nadia quickly clicked to a different screen.

Her boss snarled up to her desk, muttering about a missing folder or last-minute detail. Somehow, it was her fault, as always. He spewed insults like spittle as he snatched the folder and rushed out the door again.

Through the glass doors, Sheila and Nadia watched him walking the unnatural pace of someone who was late but refusing to run. He turned his head slightly to the left to look at his watch, just as his right foot landed in the dog mess on the pavement. He took two more steps and pulled his roller suitcase over it as well, before he smelled it. The girls watched him shouting upsets and insults, lashing out at anyone around.

Protected by the glass and the revolving door, they smothered their laughter and looked down at their keyboards, as if they had seen nothing.

AT THE END of the day, Nadia left work behind and stepped out into the late summer sun. She smiled to herself. Yes, she was going to change. Confidence would come emanating from her, as soon as she got that shirt. She was not going to let people walk all over her. She put on her sunglasses and looked up to the sky. The polarized lenses put a pink trim all around the clouds. There were so many great possibilities ahead, for anyone who had the courage to–

At the last moment she side-stepped the remaining dog mess, already decorated by multiple tread marks.

It wouldn't work to always look optimistically skywards. You had to be sure of where your feet would land, especially around here. She would try again to be that woman, once the H&M package arrived. Actually, maybe she'd start right now.

Free to Lie in Bed as if Waking-up-Time Will Never Come

Eamon Somers

It was her I noticed first, bending over four pieces of luggage taking up so much room on the floor of the resentfully packed East bound Hammersmith & City line train. I'm glad to be out of the afternoon rain and to get a seat. He is looking at his phone with his back to the carriage's double doors while she is rummaging in one of their two black backpacks. Her yoga-like forward bend causes her t-shirt, also black, to ride up and reveal a remarkably slim, symmetrical, and deeply tanned waist.

Except for the welcome white slash of the soles of her trainers and the shared discreet logo in a contrasting shade on their trainers, backpacks, and the bicep cuffs of their t-shirts, all their visible possessions are black. The sports company doesn't need my help to be famous, so I won't mention their name.

His only movement during the journey to Liverpool Street station was his phone scrolling finger. Whereas she was in perpetual motion, reaching first for the overhead flexible grip before transferring to the fixed higher bar, then switching her hold from her right hand to her left, followed by squeezing with both hands and swaying slightly as if she was a trapeze artist waiting to launch herself into the air to be caught by her colleague already swinging towards her.

Perhaps she was bored, trying to find comfort, was seeking attention, or displaying her defiance after an exchange of angry words, with someone, maybe him. Even when the seat nearest to her became vacant at Euston Square and she sat down, she immediately began to wriggle as if looking for a position that satisfied her, or was exploring sleeping positions and acting out something from her dream, some inner turmoil; concern about the trip ahead, the trip they were finishing, or even the trade exhibition they might have been working at all day, selling their sportswear to wannabe athletes who think it's the clothes that make the two of them so fit looking. Was I looking at two thirty-something champions? The evidence is circumstantial, my interpretation based on her ants-in-the-pants and teenage-like movements, suggesting she longed to be jumping over hurdles, smashing tennis returns, or tumbling across gymnastics mats. It's what I do; imagining the lives of the strangers I observe, it's a freedom I take for granted, just as you can reject my caricatures, and ask questions about my, possibly darker, motives.

It was when he picked up the nearest backpack and stretched it towards her that I noticed his smartwatch, black, and then hers, not black but grey. Otherwise clearly from the same stable, the watch faces are textured like tiny raffia mats.

He nodded his head towards the doors when they opened and waited for her to hoist the backpack before he handed her one of the holdalls. Then I was on the platform looking for the signs to tell me the way to the National Rail exit, while simultaneously trying to monitor their progress through the packed platform. He, slightly in front of her, and me checking his latest nod for meaning, until I see he was indicating the sign I might have followed if I hadn't already committed myself to the one pointing in the opposite direction. I am pleased to get away from them, I have all I need to construct a narrative to satisfy my creative impulses.

Is it obvious I don't like him? I can see she might be a bundle of dangerous energy, and his wordless instructions, "take the bag, follow me," could be the managing strategies he's found work best whenever she's like this. Whatever 'like this' means. I'm not obliged to love him, even if I ignore evidence to suggest he's a nice person. I can feel however I want about him.

I will make them a unit, their family of choice, he, finding purpose in managing and corralling her when necessary; she, happy to have him as her rock as she deals with her inner turmoil. He may find it all too much sometimes, and she may occasionally think she'd be happier with someone at least as hyperactive as she is. But they will come back to each other. I want this to be prairie-sized story, wide with possibilities, and not some sad little tale of control and resistance or even acceptance. They are a unit. They will die as old people, unless he puts her out of her misery, or she goes too far and strangles him. I see her vice-like thighs around his neck squeezing, squeezing, possibly with a pillow over his face, but I will have to research pillows and stuff if that is how it will end. The only restriction is my imagination. My interaction with my keyboard will fill their lives with obstructions or allow them more fulfilment than I currently think they deserve. In the material world, they can only be the people they are, bound by the choices they have already made. But I can take them anywhere.

Did I mention his shorts? No, I didn't, I am playing here, giving myself permission to return to my earlier descriptions of them, and to belatedly mention his legs, every bit as tanned as the portion of back revealed when her t-shirt rode up as she bent over to do whatever she was doing in her backpack. I am drawing attention to my failure to mention the shorts earlier, and to the fact that I am doing so now, and deliberately linking his tanned legs to her tanned back.

I'm supposed to be a gay man, so should I or more interestingly why did I not respond immediately to seeing his naked legs? Perhaps I was stopped by their ordinariness, their lack of development, the obvious absence of strong manly sinews? Not all sporting activities improve the shape of a man's legs, but that's not important here. It was the unexpected sight of this woman's straight-legged bend, rather than a squat, her trousered bum inches from my sitting self, and topped by her slim tanned waist. A sight generally foreign to me, at least in comparison to how often I notice bare legs on men.

I won't feel misunderstood if you reject my interpretations. This is a made-up story. Some of it is true, and some is something else, although within the context of my writing, it is all true. I am not the "I" of the story, and they are not (let's give them names) the Lauren and James of the story.

"Maybe, but doesn't a story need to go somewhere in order for it to be a story?" I hear a voice; yours, my own, or Lauren's, on repeat; "where the f**k is this going?"

I will not put them in bed together. But if you do, I sense you will engineer it so I am there also, part of a triangle, torn between my natural interest in men, and my surprising fascination with Lauren's lower back and waist. Me perhaps standing away from the bed, watching, but engaged, unless I hijack my assigned role and recast myself as their live-streaming cameraman. James is statuesque, or somehow contained, unmoved, though naked and ready. Lauren is rolling about looking for the perfect position, struggling to remember how she can best present herself, whether she should let him see the bits of her he likes best, or should hide them until he begs. Surely, they are performers. And if I examined their bed linen, would I find the sports company's logo emerging from the sheets' dark folds?

The Stansted train was predictable, sadly surrounded as I was by much less interesting stimulation, and not helped by James coming on to me, and randomly telling me Lauren and I shared an interest in choral music. Too much going on, I needed to put them away, to let them ferment privately until I am ready to commit them to paper. I did my best to switch my mind to my flight and my parents fussing over my anticipated arrival in Malaga. When I got to my crowded departure gate I sat and watched passengers boarding, frozen, my only movement being the blinking of my eyes. I was still there when the plane was reversed out of its bay. A low-sized man pushing a cleaner's trolly offers me a paper towel and asks if I am ok. 'My parents were always old, were never anything like Lauren and James,' I say. He shakes his head, smiles, and pushes on. I make my way back to London, the moist paper towel scrunching in my trouser pocket.

As this story is less about the couple on the train and more about me, then it must circle back to me, loaded now with ammunition to raise doubts about my certainties.

I am an artist who cleaves limpid like to verifiable facts, while indulging my wish to interpret those facts any way I like. Even so, I must report that a whispering voice is telling me that moments before the woman bent over inches from my face and diverted my attention from whatever I was thinking about, I might have heard someone in the carriage say; 'how far is it from Stepney Green to Mile End?' And assuming this is not a false recovered memory, then it was he who asked, and it was she who responded, which may cause a reader to question my assertion that he guides her through life with nods and a masculine insistence that she follows where he leads.

The Hermit
Samuel Dodson

For Eury, the next days were harsh under the sun, lapping at small pools of dying streams kept shaded by a hardy tree: all needles and no fruit. The sores on his mule worsened. He took half the belongings hanging from the poor beast's hide and tossed them beneath a cairn of stones that showed a rough path to the top of some bony peak.

On the fourth day, as the breath in his lungs began to feel coarse in the dryness of his throat, he spied a thin trail of smoke rising among the low hills. With his palm, he slapped and beat the mule, urging it onwards into the low valley and up the far slope. At last, as the evening sun dipped, their long shadows fell at the mouth of a cave. Where, a filthy man in rags, with whispers of greased hair falling from his liver-spotted bald head, was sitting beside a meagre fire.

'Your smoke,' Eury said when the man's face didn't move to acknowledge him. 'Is it to be our salvation or will you shun us on to die on these parched hills?'

The old man said nothing. Moved not an inch. Across the small flames a rodent was spitted. It had been skinned poorly and its fur was blackened and singed, but to Eury it looked like half a great feast. If only he could find water.

'So you mean to kill us, then?' Eury prompted. 'I shouldn't need to remind you it's a black mark against any man to refuse to help a guest – especially those in need. The gods themselves –'

'What gods?' The hermit spat. 'Yours? Or those I keep?'

'The gods of the Argives, of course.'

'Your gods, then,' the hermit said. 'Tell me, boy, if you honour your gods so much, do you not think I could be Pallas Athene, disguised as this old wretch to test you?'

'Of course,' Eury said. 'But it is because I know the gods that I'm sure you mean to help us, if that were the case. For they like to test men, it is true, and treat us cruelly when they must. But they would find no sport in killing a feeble playwright and his poor mule.'

Fat fell from the spitted rodent and an ember flared. The old hermit scratched his filthy chin and turned the spit. Then he rose, turned, and entered the small den that was tucked into the mouth of a shallow cave. Eury followed.

Inside: all shadow, the smell of earth and stale sweat. A broken tripod cauldron was propped against the far wall. Beside them, a pile of hides served as a bed.

The hermit shuffled through the gloom, his head bent, revealing large cysts protruding beside the vertebrae of his neck. He pointed to a ring of stones that encircled a pitiful well. Eury fell at once to his knees and reached his arm down into the black hole until he felt the cool surface of the water. He cupped his hand and lifted what he could to his mouth. The water was rusty, but he licked his hand dry and went to reach down again for more. The hermit kicked him in the shoulder and sent him to the floor.

'You think you can just drink my water without payment?' He peeled his lips back.

'Sir,' Eury said, 'I have nothing to offer – save my mule, who is weak and in sore need of care. What can I give?'

'You think I am a man in dire need of feckless things?' the old man replied. 'Of possessions and belongings that clutter a man's home and mind? You said you were a playwright, boy? To look at you, I doubt it. So, I ask you to fill my home and mind with words and stories – not with nonsense.'

Eury tasted the salt in his saliva. The mule outside brayed. He tried to conjure the memories of watching the actors reciting the words of Homer as he stood beside his father and gripped his hand, but in his thirst all he could recall was the pressure of his father's grip, the callouses of his worked fingers folded around his own small things. He longed for some great hand to hold his now and show him the way.

'Sir,' Eury said. 'You are a man after my own heart. I can see you are wise. Who can value words above possessions and not be so? But I am so parched. A man of your experience must know no actor or playwright can perform with a mouth as dry as salt. Please – I beg you – a bowl of water and some for my mule outside, so I am not brought to distraction by concern for his welfare. He is a good beast after all, and our troubles have been shared together.'

The hermit grunted. He picked up a large bowl and handed it to Eury, who seized it eagerly, reaching into the well and filling it, then lifting to his lips and draining it quickly. The taste of iron on his lips was a small price to pay and he paid it gladly. He was impressed by his own wits and words and thought he ought to write them down, when he had the parchment and ink to do so. He knew, though – like all writers do – that his inspired verse would appear cold and dull as soon as it was committed to papyrus.

As the hermit took a bowl to the mule outside, Eury composed himself. He found that his eyes came to focus on the wall of the cave, where shadows from the fire outside fell and seemed to shift and dance in such a way that soon he was looking not at shadows, but at the great heads of Scylla, leathery and scaled with a triple row of sharp fangs in her gory mouth. She was reaching from her desolate crag to pluck the finest of Odysseus's men from their black ship, hurling them screaming to the air, the calls for their mothers, for past lovers, for mercy, half lost amid the tearing of their flesh and the crashing of great waves against the rock, and the gurgling, insatiable roar of the monster herself, desperate for infamy and blood – so much blood: the blood flushing from her cave and onto the flint beneath her feet, towering above the sailors below, each of them with shit in their pants and piss running down their legs, pulling desperately at the oars as the great snaking heads of Scylla searched out their comrades. All the while, Odysseus, supposedly the god-like hero, but in truth just like the rest, pulling on his armour and screaming for his men to pull him to safety, as the traces of his last meal seeped down his inner leg.

It was this story Eury spun for the hermit when he returned to the den and sat beside the well. As he spoke, he felt the winged words of Homer himself, rising from his tongue and springing from his lips. The hairs on his neck pricked and he could feel an energy he remembered from the days he spent inventing far-off lands with Neo, as they sat beside quiet streams, listening to the babble.

His tale finished, he breathed deeply and looked at the hermit.

'I've heard better.' The old man uncrossed his legs and rose up and began bothering with bits in his hovel.

'Sir?' Eury said.

'You have a question?' The hermit asked. 'Or do you want something else? Your source material is weary and old, and your telling of it full of cliché. You think you can live to my age and not hear the same story told by the same young men who all think they can be poets and playwrights just because their doting mothers told them their stories made them weep? Still, yours is payment enough for the water. To have some of this squirrel, though, you must learn to be less damned derivative.'

The hermit's words hung in the air as he went outside and picked the charred rodent off its sorry spit. He took the mule by its reigns and brought it through the tattered fabric that hung across the cave's entrance. With it inside, he began examining the mule's sores as he took a bite from the squirrel's stomach.

'I'm sorry my story disappointed,' Eury said. He clenched his fists by his side and felt once more a child, scolded by his father, or clipped by the housekeeper at his lord's estate, for some transgression. Heat sprang at the base of his neck, though he was far from the fire.

'Disappointed?' the hermit said. 'No. Not disappointed. *Disinterested*. A far worse failing of a story.'

'Then perhaps I should be honest, sir,' Eury said, half fighting back tears he had not shed in years. 'You are the first audience for my stories other than my parents, and my young friends at my new lord's palace.'

At these words, the man stopped at his task. He was applying a clever paste to the wounds of the mule. He set it down and approached Eury. The boy was surprised when he placed a hand on his shoulder.

'If that is true young man, that I am your first audience to witness your stories as a stranger, then it is an honour.'

'An honour to witness such a failure, you mean? Or some other feat of indignity?'

'Not at all,' he said. 'An honour to be a part of such a moment. A privilege, even, to be the first to tell you the truth, plainly. That yours is a voice true enough, but too inclined to thievery – stealing and reporting the same old words of your forebears. Greece has had enough of the old yarns: it needs something different, something *new*. No more talk of men blessed by gods to do impossible things – but of the truth of the world as it is.'

'And what is the truth of the world?' Eury replied.

'Whatever your truth is, of course. What is true in your private heart is true for all men.'

Eury thought for a while. He brought his hands from his sides and unfurled his fingers. Outside, the embers of the fire sparked.

'But what truth of mine can I share with you, old man? That I was brought little better than a slave to my new master after my father's bad bets? That I set out from my lord's house with three friends, but became separated from them, spending days burnt by the sun and driven to your squat by our desperation and thirst?'

'Superficialities,' the hermit dismissed.

'Then perhaps I should tell you instead that, after all these years, I still wake in the mornings thinking I will see from my window our grove of olives, perhaps even spy my father spreading the sheets beneath their branches to catch them as they fall in harvest. But instead I see only the four orange walls of my sad, lonely room?' Eury half cursed the words as he rounded on the wretched old man. Spittle flew from his lips and, in that moment, he felt he had grown a foot taller. He realised with his hands he could beat the hermit, wring his neck, or break his body. Yet all that strength he felt was channelled into his tongue, which poured out his heart.

'Or perhaps you would like to know that I loved my father? Or that now I hate him, and will never forgive him for sending me off as though I were only one more possession of his to be bartered? Would you like me to tell you the first person I thought of after I bedded a woman for the first time was the king's son, Neo, or that I should like to cut my own balls off for forgetting that pretty girl's name? That all I remember of her is her perfume, and the softness on my fingers as I touched her? That nothing else but the sound of some lyre being played by some scrounging bard nearby even touches my memory?'

'Maybe I should tell you that I have not eaten oranges since those we ate that evening, Neo and I, sheltering from a sudden summer storm beneath the branches of an oak tree. The oranges were so full of juice that it spilled down our chins and covered our fingertips. The rain overhead fell through the leaves and struck our skin as we tore through that fruit. For me, there is nothing I can remember more clearly than that taste and the smell of fresh rain striking the dry grass nearby.'

'Or is it just that even now, as a man standing before you, I would like to yell and call for my mother – that I would give everything for her to be with me now? Is that truth enough for you, old man?'

Eury's words seemed captured by the old walls of the cave, and for a moment the only sounds he could hear were the heavy breathing of the mule, and the beating of his own heart.

As the shadows of the flames from the fire continued to dance on the wall, the hermit simply reached across to Eury and handed him the spit with the roasted meat.

'Now,' he said, 'you've earned your bit of squirrel.'

Fluid Dynamics
Ivy Ngeow

Yamaguchi picked up eight croissants, a bag of coffee beans and a box of berries in a Tokyo deli near the harbour before he made his way to the Yokohama Bayside Marina. The marina was well-sited between Tokyo Bay and the ocean. A sunny and chilly spring day was a perfect day on the water. He stared at his shopping basket. He didn't want ground coffee, or a cup of takeaway, when there was a grinder on the boat. For some reason he thought harder about this than he should. There was always that slight fear: what if the grinder was not working and neither his wife nor the robotics told him?

He re-tied the dogs' leashes to a railing and went back into the shop to purchase a bag of ground coffee too. That should do it. A backup was always necessary. Before boat trips, his wife usually took care of the weekend meals. And their three sons and two shiba inu dogs. Often there was delightful food for the family, like wagyu or prawns for dinner. Chilled Chablis. There was also dry dog food in the kitchen cabinets. Wives did that. Details. This time she had taken the boys on vacation to the mountains, and it was his first time alone on the new roboboat with the dogs, Yuki (fortune) and Adzuki (red bean).

A few years ago, robotics designer Akira Yamaguchi decided that he needed a better boat, since he was just an okay and not a great skipper. And even if he was, weekends and holidays were important to him. He had to relax and he couldn't. The cockpit of his previous 11-metre deck had been a continuation of a place of work. He could not stop. While family, friends and the dogs were lounging on deck or swimming, he worried about parking, steering, driving and even letting it drift. And that was in the summer. In the dreaded worse months of the year, it was enough to stop him going to sea.

He climbed onto the deck and Yuki, the braver of the dogs, leapt across, while he picked up and carried Adzuki in like a toddler. 'Let's go, guys,' he said to the dogs. He took his backpack of food off. He liked the sun on his face. A moment passed as he felt the simple salty burn of wind on his skin that cold spring day. He felt alive. A boat was not a car which, when parked, was stationary. Dead. Immobile. Asleep or active, a boat was living. A pleasant moment could turn into disaster in a matter of minutes depending on the mood of the sea. His dogs barked abundantly at something on the horizon but he had no idea what was killing them. Sometimes they did go manic if they heard or saw something that humans weren't aware of, or if they had too much pent-up energy.

He'd learned much from his dogs.

He unlocked the cabin with the app code on his phone. On the rare occasion he did not have a phone, battery life or signal, the security also worked. There was a manual override. Voice activation and fingerprint. Yamaguchi thought of the backups in every situation. Robots knew voice and touch. But they did not read minds or hearts. That did not bother him since people didn't either. Predictability was all in a day's work in robotics engineering.

Owning a boat was a symbol of one's wealth and status, not only in Japan but throughout the world. It was a luxury pastime, an asset, even if you still had to do the luxurious work of manning the cockpit. You could build years of experience or hire a crew but Yamaguchi didn't want either. He didn't have time.

Now he did. He unpacked in the kitchen. He removed just a couple of croissants, leaving the rest in the paper bag which he left inside the backpack. The grinder worked. It came as a surprise, like sun after a storm. Of course it would work. He turned on the tap and filled the coffee machine with water.

As founder of Tokyo's Robert Lab, he used his wife's connections from her various luxury food-related businesses in Taiwan. There was no one called Robert, Yamaguchi had said in the most recent Dezeen interview. It was *robot* in Japanese slang, being similar sounding words. The press had dubbed his new invention the Roboboat. Every item or nickname now linked to him started with Rob yet his name was not Rob or Robert or Robot. It soothed him to be in control and gave him the same sense of satisfaction as sticking a sticker onto a present he'd wrapped beautifully, one that he also made himself. A feeling of *done*.

Time for breakfast. He watched the dogs go off sniffing and exploring. They'd been on the roboboat twice before but sniffing was part of their peace, their enjoyment of space. He placed both croissants carefully onto a plate. He could easily eat them all day. Light, buttery and full of air. He'd looked at the other pastries in the deli but didn't feel like any of them. He also didn't want ham or cheese which would have given him an upset stomach on the sea. He stuck to plain as he was avoiding sugar.

Unlike his wife.

Yamaguchi's wife introduced him to Heavenly Treats, a sweet manufacturing powerhouse run by young engineer and entrepreneur Huang Liang. Long-haired and charismatic, the top-hatted Taiwanese was also an absolute genius. An artist. A yoghurt maker. A kiosk constructor. There was seemingly nothing he could not do. In Taiwan they called him Johnny Depp. They meant Willy Wonka. The Taiwanese mostly had a sweet tooth, a sense of humour and a ready-made, eager audience. With their street desserts popular throughout Asia, judging by the queues at self-driving kiosks, restaurants and cafes were increasingly outdated. The concept of the light and functional semi-automated kiosks was Taiwan's dessert business model. Bureaucracy was thin, so they built things fast.

Build me a kiosk that's a boat, a boat that's a kiosk, was what Yamaguchi seemed to recall saying to Huang Liang three years ago, and it was quoted in Forbes and Scientific American, so it must be true. *A yacht that was yoghurt.* Cute, small, organic and fun. He told Scientific that aesthetically, the design was not inspired by Italian or worse still, Middle Eastern sensibilities. He steered (ha!) clear of ornamentation, over-design and over-specification. The 12-metre boat had rounded edges and a bulbous bow. The profiles of other vessels in this class were angled, pointed, just like their European owners' sleek profiles. Yamaguchi said the design of the boat was Japanese through and through. He wanted to reflect that traditional, simple and clean lifestyle still being practised today. A sense of order. A sense of calm. What the world knew of as Japanese.

He did not mention Taiwanese.

After all, boat-building would have just been boat-building without Robert lab. Why else would it be called The Japanese Roboboat? Not *a*, but *the*.

Yamaguchi's father, a now retired engineer, always encouraged him to find an intelligent and educated woman. *You see,* his father had said, *a marriage is an address book. It has personal and work contacts for life.* When you see your wife eating a lot of frozen yoghurts, you must find out why. Okay. His father didn't say that but he could imagine him saying it; smell a lead when it's close to home. *Also, please, my most esteemed, dear son, marry someone from home. No foreigner will be able to put up with our customs. How could someone understand the 14 levels of formality unless they were Japanese?*

Yamaguchi and his wife secured funding and founded Robert Lab X, a joint venture with Huang Liang. On a gritty, windy winter's day in an Osaka boatyard, The Roboboat, the kiosk boat or Kioboat was finally born. There were many nicknames, press names, but the boat would always be revered and known as the Inuyasha to Yamaguchi.

Inuyasha was the name of a classic popular fantasy anime and manga series written and illustrated by Rumiko Takahashi. Inu was dog in Japanese, and yasha was wild soul or demon. The main character, Kagome, was a 15-year-old girl in contemporary Tokyo who was transported to another world in the past and met the dog-demon named Inuyasha.

At last, Yamaguchi was in control without being at the controls. A real Captain. A Captain's Captain. The Inuyasha concept was his idea of what a cruiser should be. 'A companion in a quest, like you guys,' he muttered absent-mindedly to the dogs.

With two bedrooms, a kitchen, solar power, a bathroom with shower, handbasin and toilet it was as neat and compact as the first Heavenly Treats kiosk that he set his eyes on. But all this was immaterial. It was the self-driving that lowered the Captain's stress levels. The GPS enabled the boat to remain stationary without an anchor. A stabilising gyroscope device, nicknamed Kagome by Yamaguchi's son, reduced rolling and jerking to a gentle bob at a switch. *Animism*, his son had said, *is a form of superstition. Even the joystick must have a name.*

They set sail. Without his family around, he'd planned and programmed the route for that day, for open and base waterways, not the middle of the ocean. Inuyasha was driving herself, cruising around Tokyo. A day trip. Naturally the dogs also drove themselves, as they did always. When they finished their nasal explorative journey, they lay down in the shade on the deck, always near Yamaguchi.

It was time to relax. The point was that he could spend time with his family and friends while the robot drove the boat and looked after every necessity. He didn't even need to step into the cockpit. Yet he did. He'd rather eat in the cockpit than on the clean pine kitchen countertop. He'd rather make crumbs, he thought as he stared at the ironic joysticks and dials. It would give him something to clean up.

Why was his wife on vacation in the mountains? Why Taiwan? He knew why. Right now she would be tunnelling through a 11-mile long canyon trip up the marble walls of the Taroko Gorge. The twisting, soaring feature of Taroko National Park. They would have cruised the LiWu river. He looked all this up or rather he got his office droid Charlesbot to look it all up and read it back to him the moment she'd mentioned the trip a month ago. Charlesbot was good like that. He was not Google. He could give an opinion that would be very similar in syntax and content to Yamaguchi, who did not want a female android. That would seem perverted. Why not instead have a "buddy" type android? Humorous, sarcastic, truthful. All the things a buddy should be. Not some girl who said witty things. He already had a wife who did that. And look what happened.

Charlesbot was a prototype level 3, and still, a work-in-progress. All works of art are. Nothing lasts, nothing is finished, nothing is perfect. Wabi Sabi is the ancient Japanese wisdom of finding beauty in imperfection and simplicity in nature. If you could have a companion in your quest who knew what you wanted to know, but better that you knew yourself, wouldn't you? Most of us were afraid of the truth. It did not sound very good. So why not have some bot-honest light humour with a moral touch, appropriate to your cultural context instead? Charlesbot, also designed and made in Robert Lab, was a cross between a priest, and a Wes Anderson movie. Yamaguchi had taken Charlesbot to the China Hi-Tech Fair (CHTF) in Shenzhen several years ago and met other droids such as Nick, Alisha and Gerry on the international "droid playdate" scene. The robotics engineers and their droids stayed at the Four Seasons, where the organisers and sponsors threw parties to make sure they'd had a good time. Yamaguchi remembered the droids' names and even what they looked like and said, but nothing about the engineers came back to him.

Yamaguchi now had a waiting list for more Inuyasha Roboboats to be made for the ultra-rich. The price tag was 1.2m euros but at least 5 people were waiting for them to be born in the Osaka boatyard while Robert Lab worked on the AI. Quite a few people, it seemed, wanted a stress-free cockpit experience.

Back at the Lab, Charlesbot had said to him, 'Just picture Huang

Liang with his long hair in a man bun, the top hat discarded for all-weather high visibility gear and some made-in-China hiking boots.'

Yamaguchi imagined that his oldest son would be forced to put his Nintendo down for a vintage train trip at Xinchen or Hualien, the same boy who came up with the manga names of Kagome for the joystick and Inuyasha for the vessel, and the dogs' names, who wrote and illustrated his own manga graphic novels before he realised he didn't like them that much, and it was a saturated market. The athletic middle son who could disappear like a ghost and only wanted food, shed loads of it, from his mother. And his youngest. Just like the mother. Yankees fan, sweet-toothed and sweet-natured but with a tiger's roar inside.

And he agreed? Of course he agreed. He was not *that* kind of Japanese man. He did not own her.

He had replied to Charlesbot, 'She is not a droid, unlike you. I could have her address books, her Heavenly Treats, our Osaka boat yard, even Inuyasha the roboboat, but not *her*.'

'Oh, fuck the wagyu,'" said Charlesbot.

His father in all his sagely demeanour with business wisdom from thousands of years could not have predicted that an address book had a shelf-life, as relationships did. Anyway, he had started to get frail, and was having blood tests and so on. Who knew if his father was going to be well or unwell? So much of life depended on health, not wealth. He could not navigate the boat nor his wife, his wife who was so intelligent, whom he met in New York in college, and a fellow engineer and businesswoman. She was interested in everything, the children, the dogs, food and wine, of course, business and especially his projects at work. She was just not interested in him.

The dogs came over to be patted, or so he thought. But they were only licking and vacuuming the croissant flakes dropped from a greater height of his own paws and chin onto his knees, lap, everywhere. He could hear heavy breathing and snorting as he glazed over the cockpit's dashboard, the floor, all the glittering lights, dials, knobs, counters.

Inuyasha the dog-demon silently cruised Tokyo's waterways like a ghost, while Yamaguchi retired onto the deck chair with a cup of fresh ethical Ethiopian blend. The business buzz, that entrepreneurial energy again. An ethical kiosk idea? Ideas tired him. They did not spark joy.

He used his laptop to change the route.

Leaving the cockpit, the crumbs the dogs hadn't snuffled up, he glanced back at Kagome the gyroscopic joystick, the canine breath-steamed lights, the dials. Wabi sabi. Alone, time and space and even his trash were his.

He lay reading two novellas he bought at a train station in the last month. It took at least a few hours. He did not even understand what the hell they were about. One more croissant and whiskey on ice for lunch. He became drowsy. If he could even drift away, he might get to Hawaii.

"Where the flow carries a large quantity of water, the speed of the flow is greater and vice versa." - Leonardo da Vinci.

He liked the vice versa bit most, but only because he had to think harder than he ought to, like when buying the ground coffee.

WHEN HE WOKE UP, he tossed the incomprehensible train station novellas onto the deck.

Yamaguchi stumbled out of his deck chair in a heap, like a pot plant overturned. In the kitchen, he retrieved his backpack. Inside, the paper bag was empty. The dogs had eaten all six of his remaining croissants. He cursed, crushing the paper bag and putting it in the recycling pedal bin his wife had so carefully lined. Half of his box of berries had been munched on. They'd made a glittering blood-red mess in his laptop bag, dark and shiny as wet jewels.

He took the leftover mashed berries onto the deck and flung them over the railings, box and all. Was it not organic, eco, bamboo? Deep red juice sprayed his Polo shirt. Clutching his stomach, Yamaguchi only just noticed that the novellas he'd been reading were scattered like leaves on the deck, the corners mangled and chewed by the same culprits. Picking the thin paperbacks up, he hurled them one at a time into the sea. He didn't hear a splash.

He went back to sleep on his deckchair, curled like a blood-splattered bird, not wanting to be awake when the boat arrived in the middle of the ocean.

On the Brushes
Sue Clark

I'm told my mother was a good mother. For the short time she stuck around. I can't comment, being only twenty-one months old when she decided she'd had enough and ran off. I never felt hard done by. As far as I was concerned, that Nationwide under-manager was welcome to her. I had Dad, and Dad was brilliant.

People say that all the time don't they? In cheesy cards and on cheap coffee mugs. 'Best Dad in the universe.' 'World's top Pops.' The difference is, my dad really *was* the best: fun, affectionate, energetic and, most of all, creative. He painted like an angel, although he'd never been to art school or even taken evening classes. He could just do it. Misty landscapes. Tick. Fruit so luscious you wanted to take a bite out of the paper. Tick. Exquisite flowers and butterflies that seemed to flutter in an invisible breeze. All delicately done in subtle watercolours. Surprising really for a big man like my dad, with big, sausage fingers.

If he had a fault – and I'd argue it was the world that was at fault, not Dad – it was that his art brought him little material reward. That is to say, we were poor. Dad wasn't even able to pick up much casual work to supplement what he made from his art because, labelling conventional schooling 'stifling', Dad taught me at home.

Not so much taught, if I'm honest. More, that he let me soak up experiences. He never sat me down in front of a pile of textbooks and commanded me to read them. More often than not, we were out walking the fields or driving around in Dad's old banger. I learnt about science from the trees, clouds and stars. I learnt about maths by counting the legs on a centipede and the spots on a ladybird. I learnt to read and write in trips to the little town library. Most of all, I learnt about art by watching at his elbow as he swept a paintbrush across white paper.

We were content but life could be hard. Though Dad's translucent landscapes and fragile flower paintings were magic to me, hardly anyone else appreciated them. Every week we'd set out in the car, doing the rounds of the smaller galleries and gift shops in the area, only to return in the evening, dad's broad shoulders and my narrow ones slumped, portfolio case full of unsold pictures.

Then one day, we had a breakthrough.

Dad got chatting to a woman wearing a man's peaked cap, selling fruit and veg at the Excellence Market. I watched them from behind a display of artisan cheeses. After a while, I saw him extract one of his still-lives from the case and hand it over. She examined it. Then I heard her say, 'Them grapes look like they've just been picked from the vine. And I should know. Here, why don't you get yourself a stall? You'd sell way more that way.'

Dad took a stall the following week. For several months, our fortunes looked up. Sales were good, then steady, then faltering. Finally, they tailed off to almost nothing. 'Think people are fed up with my fields, fruit and flowers,' he told me. 'I heard one bloke say they were corny. Time for a rethink.'

With the wisdom of a twelve-year-old, I offered my advice. 'Don't worry Dad. All great artists struggle. Then when they die – guess what? – their paintings are on tea towels, fridge magnets, key rings and I don't know what. They're famous. Just like you will be one day. I know it.'

Dad's smile was kind but sad. 'Can't wait till "one day", my girl. Got bills to pay. Urgent action is needed.'

I WOKE next morning to find Dad had gone. He'd left a note on the kitchen table: 'Off to get a proper job.' Next to the note was a copy of the local newspaper. A small ad was circled in emphatic biro: *We're hiring! Drivers wanted. Apply in person to East Oxon Bus Company.*

All day I waited and worried, unable to settle to any of my usual chores: fashioning paintbrushes out of foraged badger hair, stretching paper ready for the paint, cataloguing reference photos. By the time Dad came home late that afternoon, I was beside myself.

Grey with weariness, he collapsed into his armchair. Over at the sink, I froze, tea-towel in hand, anxious for myself, and him. How would he cope with yet another rejection? But when he looked up, he was beaming.

'I got it girl. I got the job. Start training next week. They said I had exceptional observational abilities. What do you think about that then, eh?' He stood and lifted me off my feet. 'Your old dad's gonna be a bus driver,' he shouted. 'Ding! Ding!'

'You can't,' I called down prissily from somewhere near the ceiling. 'You're an artist.'

He plonked me on the ground. 'Don't you come all hoity-toity with me, my girl. It's good, honest work and, think of it, I'll have the freedom of the road under my wheels all day long.'

HOW I LAUGHED the morning he came downstairs in his stiff, new uniform, hair slicked back, shoes polished, ready to start his first shift!

'Bit of a change from worn-down slippers and paint-splattered overalls,' I said, still not sure this was a good idea.

'You could do with smartening up yourself, come to think of it,' Dad said, shooting me a look. 'With me out at work all day, it's about time you went to school. Can't have you lollygagging about the place while I'm grafting.'

So Dad went on the buses and I went to the town comp up the road. Amazingly, we both took to our new roles.

'No boss breathing down my neck and, at the end of the month, a nice pay packet,' he said. 'Though some of the passengers can be right pains-in-the-whatsit. Had one old dear today wanting to pay me with a twenty-pound note. I ask you!'

I soon got the hang of school, once I remembered to put my hand up before I spoke, brush my hair every morning, and keep my shoes on all day. Dad may not have been much cop on kings and queens, and quadratic equations, but he did teach me to listen and to look. I listened and I looked and I learned. A lot. Enough to pass the exams and, eventually, get into university.

Meanwhile, Dad had money in his pocket and a bunch of new mates to have a pint with on a Friday night. He'd gained a lot but what he'd lost was more precious: his creative urge. He tried several times but wildflower meadows and bowls of fruit no longer excited him. Months passed when he didn't so much as pick up a paintbrush.

Then one day, he came home carrying a bulging shopping bag and wearing a big smile.

'Acrylics,' he said, unpacking the bag of paint supplies. 'They're the thing, I hear. Lot more depth. Lot more life. Let's see if the old magic is still there, shall we?'

It was. Before long, when Dad wasn't behind the wheel of a bus, he was in front of an easel. He'd found new inspiration: the general public, in all their infuriating and idiosyncratic ways, became his muse.

Morning commuters, dozing in their seats, mouths gaping. Red-faced mothers wrestling with pushchairs the size of deckchairs. Elderly ladies with too-much lipstick and sharp elbows, gruffly brushing people aside. Middle-aged couples, caught mid-row, looking blankly through each other. Young lovers, arms and legs possessively entwined. Schoolkids sneakily sticking chewing gum under their seats. They were all there in his paintings. Every ill-fitting coat and secretive hat. Every wrinkle and frown, jutted chin and bony fist. He called the series of paintings, *Passengers*.

These were not the pale and delicate artworks of before. Dad squeezed, scrubbed, scraped and smeared the paint onto the canvas in thick, audacious daubs. His subjects didn't just jump from the frame. They shot out at you with the power of a Saturn rocket. They thumped against your retina. More than one viewer took an involuntary step backward when they saw them.

At first, he sold only to his driver friends. They were tickled by the compositions, recognising the truths in these unremarkable, remarkable scenes. Then the local press sniffed out the story. 'On The Brushes: arty bus-driver changes gear' shouted the headline.

There followed a brief spot on regional TV's *This is Central* programme. Then Dad was featured in a Radio 2 breakfast show and finally the ultimate: *The One Show*. It wasn't long before Dad had trouble finding time between shifts to meet the demand for his pictures.

He struggled on, fitting his painting into the hours when he wasn't working. Staying up late. Getting up at dawn. Something had to give. One Monday morning, he handed in his notice at the bus station, shaking every single one of his co-workers by the hand before taking his leave of the East Oxon Bus Company. It happened to be half-term, so I went along as moral support.

'You've been the best of mates,' he said, wiping away a tear. 'I'll miss you, you buggers. And them blasted passengers.'

DAD HAD what he'd always wanted: the time and the means to paint. An interview with Alan Yentob followed, filmed in the bus depot he'd so recently left and in our ramshackle house, now undergoing major renovation. Dad's *Passengers* hung in London galleries and were fuzzily reproduced, as I had childishly predicted, on tea towels, key rings and fridge magnets throughout the land.

He had a glass-sided studio built at the bottom of the garden. He took on a manager and an accountant. If he wasn't in his studio turning out more *Passengers,* he was in meetings, at lunches or giving talks. His social circle moved up several rungs. He was mixing with gallery owners, dealers, curators, art critics, collectors and junior culture ministers. Grayson Perry invited himself round to tea.

By then I'd moved to London. Idly glancing at Dad's website one evening, I noticed a change. Week by week his paintings were becoming less intense, less punchy. More – dare I say it? – corny. I phoned him.

He was just back from dinner at The Ivy with the Chair of Tate Modern and a little the worse for wear. Otherwise, I doubt I'd have got the confession out of him.

'Day by day, I feel the inspiration draining from me, girl. I just don't have subjects I can get stuck into any more.'

'What about the people you mix with now,' I said. 'You could paint them. Call the series *Trendsetters.*'

'Tried that. Didn't work. They're a whey-faced lot! No personality, no grit, no life. Except Grayson, of course. But I can't paint him all the time!'

I wasn't the only one to notice the change. Sales began to slip. Dad argued with, then parted company with, first his manager, then his accountant. I watched the decline from afar.

'I need to rediscover my zest for life,' Dad told me over the phone, sounding more disheartened than I ever remembered him. 'Then maybe I'll be inspired again.'

'I assume you don't want to go the therapy route?'

'I leave all that sort of stuff to you young folk, thank you very much,' he said, as I knew he would.

'Right then. A change of scene. Move abroad. Somewhere warm. France. Italy. Somewhere snowy. The Canadian Rockies. Go on an adventure. Challenge yourself. Machu Picchu or the Himalayas. Take up sailing. Or flying. Push against the edges of your comfort zone.'

I could hear him muttering, unimpressed.

'Ok then. Sign up to Match.com. Find yourself a lady love.'

A spluttering sound came down the line.

'My last throw of the dice,' I said. 'Get a dog.'

'Thanks for the ideas, love. All made with the best intentions, I know. But I've been mulling it over and I have a simpler plan.'

He'd say no more.

Weeks went by, I was caught up in the new job. Did I say? I'm an art psychotherapist. Never had the urge to make splotches on canvas myself, though every day I see the benefit to others. I hadn't been home for months. I thought I'd surprise Dad but when I got there, he was out, and not answering his phone.

I amused myself in the house for a while then, bored, wandered up the garden to the studio. And stood in amazement. The faces of damp commuters, engrossed lovers, grumpy pensioners and cheeky schoolchildren stared back at me through the glass. The building was stacked with the most dazzlingly bright portraits. More than a dozen of them. Some finished. Some works in progress. Dad was painting again, and more vividly than ever.

I heard a sound behind me. He was home.

'Kept meaning to tell you,' he said. 'Total freedom didn't suit me, girl. I needed to get back on the buses to rediscover my mojo. I needed them pains-in-the-whatsit passengers with their sharp elbows, chewing gum, and blasted twenty-pound notes.'

As I looked at his now thinning, slicked-back hair, too-snug uniform and shiny shoes, there was only one thing left to say.

We hugged and shouted it together. 'Ding! Ding!'

Magnolia Walls
Jamie Chipperfield

The sunrise stirred me with angular shards of golden light sneaking through the cracks in my curtains, carving themselves into the walls of my childhood bedroom. Half-awake, I sighed mournfully at the day ahead. As much as I wanted to linger beneath my sheets, as I had lingered through life in general for the past twenty years, a clock that could not be silenced ticked ominously in my mind.

I chucked on clothes from the day before and headed for the kitchen. Like Old Mother Hubbard the cupboards were bare, devoid of both food and possessions. Breakfast consisted of a cup of tea, made in a travel thermos, diluted with the dregs from a pint of milk. One last cup of tea. A farewell tea. Drunk in memory to all those that had gone before. But unlike all the other gallons of tea this house had seen, this final cuppa was drunk in surroundings that were eerily unfamiliar.

Fundamentally, the kitchen was the same room it always had been, down to its very bones. The same room in the same house, built with bricks untouched since the day they were laid. Yes, it was the same house, but we respond to more than the cold facts of logic. The kitchen of old, of distant childhood, of youth, and this adult present, was long gone, replaced and modernised, all shiny and pristine, ready for its new owners. I was now no more than a stranger in someone else's home to be.

I knocked back the last of my tea, and then immediately regretted it. I could no longer resist the inevitable. Begrudgingly, I returned to my bedroom and set about dismantling my bed. A few twists of an Allen key later and it was a pile of flat-pack timber in the corner of the room. I bagged it up and left it by the front door, ready to be collected on the way out. Despite having nothing left to do in the bedroom, I found myself unable to leave, held there with all the gravitational pull of a collapsing star. A black hole of nostalgia ready to devour the unwary.

I don't know what I was expecting, the room was as it had been moments before, only emptier. The void left behind by the bed was but one of many. A Swiss cheese of departed possessions and hazy memories. Scenes played out before me like so many VHS-tinted home movies. The bedroom of my childhood and teenage years. Despite the passage of time, I remembered the room as if it were a single moment caught in amber. The vacant space now filled by a highlight reel of events and belongings from the first sixteen years of my life. A life-sized collage plucked straight from the family album.

I sneezed, and the glorious image began to crumble, fading until only the stark present remained. Once more I was standing alone in a barren room, its magnolia walls no longer adorned with any kind of identity. Sunlight seeped from the curtains, the invasive rays having shifted since I had reluctantly climbed out of bed. The room now contained only a thousand specks of dust, drifting aimlessly in the morning light.

By that point my mind was wandering, my body soon to follow. I drifted from room to room, each as empty and soulless as the last. I was meandering without purpose, shuffling along, haunting those hallowed halls like some tortured spirit.

What was I looking for? One last trip down memory lane?

Those surroundings were as familiar as the lines on the back of my hand. I could visualise each room as it had looked when still filled with life. But there was nothing left to see. I had photos, of course, the pictures on my phone taken prior to the stripping of the house, and older pictures still, taken spontaneously in the company of family and friends. But those memories now felt like ancient relics, so distant, so out of reach. Even the recent past felt like a lifetime ago. So much can change so quickly. Even after years of stagnation.

My roaming brought me to the lounge — and I froze as I stepped through the doorway. Some memories leave an indelible mark. The moments. The places. The people. The maps of our lives are drawn in permanent marker. On entering the room, I was confronted with the eternally imprinted image of my father facedown on the floor. Of course, I knew this was but a shadow of a moment from twenty years before. Here and now, the room was a blank canvas awaiting its new owners, but the stubborn, haunted past could never be scrubbed from its walls. Not for me.

I had lived eighteen years in that house before university, followed by just three years away. Two months after my return, degree in hand and the world at my feet, I found my father on the floor - and everything changed. His month-long stay in hospital, nearly dying in the process, was but a prelude to the life that came after.

Growing up is inevitable, but it moves on fast-forward when disability enters your home. Childish things are put aside, any naive ideas about the future soon abandoned. I would love to have wallowed in my youth a little longer, but there is only futility in grieving for what wasn't to be.

Twenty years of full-time care was to be my destiny. And until my father finally succumbed to his illnesses, much of that duty was spent within these four walls. Perhaps this is why my childhood memories of this place are carved into the annals of my soul, while all that followed is half-forgotten in buried trauma. The horror of watching a loved one ageing prematurely, a mind withering away before you. If there is anything to fear in this world, it is the frailty of the human mind. We are who we are only because of our capacity to think, and when that fails, what then remains of our identity?

I wrenched myself back to the present and the reality of our empty lounge, panic unfurling within. I was nauseous, sweaty, my heart thumping in my chest. And then surged a familiar feeling, something primordial telling me to get out, to take flight, to run as fast as I could. Despite the lack of tangible threat, I submitted to my instincts and fled for the nearest exit, the doors to the garden being the closest.

Fresh air hit me like a slap to the face. My heart rate began to ease and my breathing to settle. Unsure of my next move, I surrendered to the stony back step and gazed up at the morning sky. In another life I might have sobbed, but I had shed my last tears so long ago.

I had mourned for my father three times in the last twenty years, his passing being a painfully drawn-out process rather than a sudden full stop. The first time had been during his initial stay in hospital. How close he came. An unspoken forgone conclusion. It was clear enough from the nurses' expressions during visiting hours. The second time was after his discharge from hospital, returning home pursued by freshly labelled diagnoses. The relief of his survival was soon overshadowed by the discovery of the stranger who was my father. Some days, an incapable toddler, clothed in the body of an adult. Other days a raging, feral beast, beyond logic or reason. Or the worst days, when Jekyll and Hyde rotated on an hourly basis.

The third case of mourning came when he did eventually and inevitably pass. I was numb by then. There had been so many false alarms, so many times where his strength seemed to have finally faltered. But what little remained of my father after two decades of decline was a pitiful sight. By the end it was a mercy, however macabre that reality may sound. A man who had never been able to enjoy the retirement he'd worked so hard for. And all the perks that came with time being your own. Pottering around in the shed. Rainy days in the garage tinkering with cars. Summer afternoon pints in a pub beer garden. Great swathes of life. Possible no more.

My gaze drifted, settling upon my immediate surroundings. The garden looked beautiful in the morning sun. Ready for market. Like the rest of the house, it had received its fair share of renovation. Only a few afternoons of labour had made it show ready. Satisfying work. But it was bittersweet to see it, so lovely, only to bid it farewell. I had much to thank this garden for. It had been a sanctuary, a place I could escape to during my caring years. Freedom is as much a physical state of being as it is a state of mind. How easy it is to build a prison from the walls around you. But when you become a carer, or when it is thrust upon you, you are immediately deprived of liberty. Another person is now utterly reliant on you. Their needs. Their well-being. Their health. All of it now your responsibility. Like the onset of parenthood, but instead of witnessing growth and independence, you're confronted with regression and illness. Are any of us truly free to begin with, are we all just victims of fate? Are choices merely an illusion? Who we are as people if not judged by our choices? If they are choices at all.

My backside grew cold and numb on the unforgiving step. I knew had to pull myself away, the future awaited. And as much as it pained me to say a final farewell to this garden, I knew that it had to be done. Perhaps Alan Bennett said it best, in The Lady In The Van, of carers marking time, waiting for life to begin. But it is in fact we, the waiting, who are marked, by both life and time. But what he failed to mention was how we are also marked by places. As I said goodbye to the garden, to the wildlife that had visited and to the sky that had always watched over it, I understood how deeply this place had marked me.

I returned inside with a heavy heart, having delayed the inevitable long enough and began working through the remaining jobs on my mental checklist. Locking windows. Pulling blinds. Wiping surfaces. The end crept nearer with every item ticked off the list. My very own final countdown, a Damoclean sword above my head. Once the last task was accomplished, only a blank page would remain. Nothing is scarier than a blank page. How do you accept infinite possibilities when you've only ever adhered to an unyielding script?

Soon, all too soon, I found myself at the front door. With my checklist complete, there was no logical reason to linger. Behind me, in the physical sense, an empty property and its magnolia walls. Vacant and still. A melancholy epitaph to what had once been our family home. The fire of its hearth will burn again, not for me, but for new occupants, that warmth of life rising like a phoenix from our magnolia ashes. We can only go forward, propelled by what has gone before. In my case, forward meant through my former front door... and out into the world beyond.

With trepidation I took a single hesitant step into the light. The heat of the sun caressed my face, while a gentle breeze beckoned me onward. I took a forlorn look backwards through the still-open front door into the hallway and with a deep breath collected the remainder of belongings, shut the door and locked it for the final time.

The point of no return. Staring at the set of keys in the palm of my hand, I felt them suddenly as a great burden, a dead weight in my palm. Torn between clinging to a fading sense of belonging and the need to look towards an unknowable future, I sighed and lifted the letterbox flap. Ka-klink. It was done.

The heft of two black sacks in one hand and the tattered remains of my hopes and dreams in the other. The street ahead revealed an idyllic day. I steeled myself for whatever may come.

Gringos Can't Dance
Or Libertadores

PJ Whiteley

Santiago de Chile, June 1991

"When love is not madness, it is not love." – Pedro Calderón de la Barca

'It's not that warm, is it?' said Johnny, as they descended from the jumbo jet and walked across tarmac to the waiting bus. The airport buildings were colourful and low-rise, like a bus station. Johnny and Pablo rubbed their red-rimmed eyes, stumbled from the aircraft steps to the terminal.

'Well, what do you expect?' said Pablo. 'It's winter.'

'I thought winter was warm in South America.'

Pablo rolled his eyes. 'I really have to buy you a globe for your next birthday. South America's about four times the size of Europe. It stretches from the Caribbean almost to the Antarctic. Chile has every climatic zone except tropical; it has sub-tropical if you count the Juan Fernández Islands. Here in Santiago we're in a Mediterranean climate, but at the start of winter.'

'I'm very pleased for you. Thanks, geography teacher.'

'It's good to be informed.'

'It's not as smart as Buenos Aires airport,' he said.

'Everything's upside down in South America,' Pablo replied, smarting a little. 'Argentina has smart infrastructure, shaky economy. Chile is the other way around.'

'I thought your family was opposed to the regime and that.'

'Shh,' he replied. 'Anyway, it still has good businesses. Smart people. Let's not talk about the government while we're here, at least not in public places, and not 'til we know the lie of the land. Rosa says it's OK now, we're a year into democracy, but there was a wobbly couple of days in April. In any case, her side of the family is well favoured. My side ... well, not so much.'

'So, Rosa is picking us up?' asked Johnny, once they were through passport control and had picked up their back-packs.

'Yea, apparently. Scary to think of her driving.'

'Why?'

'Well, she's only 20, talks all the time. Last time I saw her was in London and she was 17. Chatty and girly, easily distracted. Can't think of her as a grown up yet. She's smart, mind, super-smart.'

'Sounds nice. We're only 19.'

'She's pretty, too. One thing about Rosa, Johnny. Don't, well you know.'

'Don't what?'

'Make moves.'

'What, are you her Dad or summat? Anyway, we might not like each other.'

'Mmm.'

'What does that mean?'

'Dunno. Gotta bad feeling. She's got a bit of a thing for guitarists. And she likes the Beatles.'

'Everyone likes the Beatles. Anyhow, she's a grown woman.'

'She's engaged, sort-of.'

'What do you mean, "sort-of?"'

'She's lined up to marry this rich guy, Arturo Ramírez, and he's away in Brazil for the family firm. Not good timing, really.'

'How can you be warning me off a girl I've never even met? Maybe I won't fancy her.'

'Oh, you will, mate. Her Dad approves the match with Arturo, and you don't want to get on the wrong side of her Dad. People who do, well....'

'They don't emerge well from the experience?'

Pablo looked at him. 'They don't emerge,' he said, flatly.

Johnny said nothing, looked at Pablo then looked around him at the other passengers. He fiddled with the stump of his missing finger, shifted his weight from one leg to the other. 'Well, I guess we're here for the match, anyway, aren't we? Confident?'

'No,' said Pablo. 'No! First time in the final for a Chilean club. Not confident at all. But *cero-cero* in the first leg, home advantage in the second. Ours to lose. Up against the Paraguayan champions. Sounds like the semi-final was awesome. Beat Boca Juniors! Wish I'd been there. Brilliant goals, pitch invasion with police and dogs, game had everything! So my cousins tell me.'

'Boca Juniors!' replied Johnny. 'They're like, big, aren't they? Maradona's old club?'

'Absolutely. So with them and the Brazilian clubs out of the way, this'll be our best chance ever. Massive game.' Pablo paused and scanned the horizon, looking for a familiar face among the jostling crowd of the Arrivals Hall. 'There she is,' he said, before adding: 'Shit.'

'What does that mean?'

'She's even prettier now. Ah well. You've been warned mate.'

'*Primaaaa!*' *Pablo shouted*. '*Que guapa eres!* How are you? All grown up and driving?' said Pablo.

'Yaaaiyy!' shrieked the attractive young woman, in mid-length designer dress, smartly cut jacket and sunglasses, throwing her hands into the air and trotting in for the hug. '*Pablo, mi primo favorito, todo inglés ahora, supongo! Que lindo que están aqui! Super-liiiindo!* And we're going to the final. Colo Colo in the final! And this must be Johnny. I've heard so much about you.'

'Likewise. You speak really good English.'

She leant in for a peck on the cheek. Johnny inhaled an intoxicating mix of expensive perfume and entitlement. There was a tingling sensation in his fingers, including the missing one.

'Thank you!' said Rosa. 'I went to the international school.'

'And you're all in Las Condes now,' said Pablo. 'Moving up in the world.'

'Dad's firm is doing well,' said Rosa, as they walked to the airport car park. 'Franchise operation, blah blah. Wants me to work for it. We'll see! Anyway, the business is making profits, that's the main thing. This regime, well, it's not so bad economically. If you manage to avoid getting shot, there are lots of opportunities.'

'They should make that the national slogan,' quipped Johnny. 'Put it on tourism posters.'

Rosa giggled. 'You're funny,' she said.

Pablo threw him a look, like he had done something wrong. Johnny widened his eyes a little with an 'I'm innocent' expression. Being funny is not flirting, his look tried to say. Oh yes it is, don't play the innocent with me, Pablo's expression replied.

'Yorkshire is the world capital of sarcasm,' explained Pablo. 'Sorry about my friend.'

'Don't apologize! I like your friend. Is Liverpool in Yorkshire, where the Beatles are from?'

'No, that's Lancashire, not far mind.'

'So, which bands are from Yorkshire?'

'Um. The Wedding Present?'

'Never heard of them. Dreadful name.'

He tried again. 'The Housemartins.'

She gave a blank look.

'Give it up, Johnny,' said Pablo, giggling. They had reached the car, threw their backpacks into the boot and climbed in, Pablo moving swiftly to the front passenger seat, leaving Johnny in the back. 'So, you can really drive?' Pablo asked her, as she drove the small Renault out of the car park and onto a broad avenue.

'Yes, yes! Don't worry, I've passed my test. I know the streets. I bet it's changed since you were last here.'
'I was five. I don't really remember.'
'Well, it's smartened up a lot. I'm going to go through the city centre. Then we can drive down O'Higgins, past the park. You can see something of the centre.'
'O'Higgins?' asked Johnny.
'Every main drag of every city, town and village the length of Chile is called O'Higgins,' explained Pablo. 'After Bernardo O'Higgins, leader of the independence movement from colonial Spain. One of the country's founding fathers. Bit like George Washington for the USA.'
'Chile got liberated from the conquistadores by an Irishman?' asked Johnny, puzzled. 'Funny old world.'
Pablo said nothing, just raised his eyes and turned his head to look out of the car window, unsure as to whether Johnny was slighting Ireland, or Chile, or Spain, or all three.
Rosa, ignoring the two lads' exchanges, was keen to be tourist guide. As they neared the city centre, she announced: 'We are now on the Avenida O'Higgins. To the left is the palace La Moneda. Then we have the main shopping centre. The cathedral is there as well. Good shops.'
Johnny followed the guide, taking in the grand Greco-Roman architecture of La Moneda, and the narrow shopping streets, some of them pedestrianized, busy with shoppers in their jackets and jeans.
'We now have a metro as well. Modern city!' Rosa beamed with pride. 'There's been a lot of progress since you were last here, Pablo.'
'Right,' said Pablo, but not with the tone of agreement.
'Pablo! We are not going to talk about politics on this visit. Lots of the good stuff is in spite of El General.'
'El Asesino, you mean,' Pablo said.
'Anyway, we have democracy now, for one year. There was a bad weekend in April when poor Jaime Guzmán got shot, but we saw it all off. I like Patricio Aylwin. He has a nice face. You can trust him.'

'*Poor* Jaime Guzmán?' asked Pablo, his temperature rising. 'You are joking. He was a member of the junta.'

'No one deserves to be shot on their way home from work. I mean, think of his family.'

'Well, his government didn't care much for ours.'

'Anyway, enough politics. We're nearly in Las Condes now.' She took one hand off the steering wheel, fiddled with her hair, while Pablo looked angrily out of the side window, and took a deep breath.

She pulled into an underground car park, beneath an apartment block. They took the elevator up to the fifth floor.

'And this is my apartment!'

'*Yours?!*' asked Pablo, incredulous, as they gazed out at the city skyline, stood in a large open plan living, kitchen and dining area, large windows on two sides giving views over the north and the west of the city.

'*Sí, primo*. You like it? There are only two bedrooms. So you and Johnny can share. But it's big!'

'It's completely yours?' he asked.

'Yes, Papa got it for me. I pay him rent. Well, sometimes.'

'When you said your Dad's firm was doing well, I didn't realise it was doing this well.' Pablo sounded admiring, nervous, daring to give himself permission to enjoy the luxury.

'Don't look so worried!' said Rosa. 'Have a beer! Let's put on some music. Juan Luis Guerra, the Beatles, Madonna, whatever.'

'Well, not Madonna,' said Pablo. He turned to Johnny: 'What was that REM song I heard on the radio when we were in the car?'

'Losing My Religion.'

'I have that album!' said Rosa, suddenly.

'Which one?'

'The REM one. Out of Time. On CD. We have a great music system here. Let's put it on.'

'Cool!' said Johnny. 'Could be worse. Modern apartment overlooking the city, ice-cold beer, REM on full blast out of Wharfedale speakers. Great company!' he glanced briefly at Rosa, who returned a warm, approving look. 'My kind of gig.'

'Welcome to the Third World!' said Pablo, laughing, raising his glass.

They slumped on the sofa.

'You're tired. You boys. You need to go to bed!'

'Not yet!' said Pablo. 'This is too cool!' He gulped down his small beer, then leapt up to fetch another, before returning to the sofa. He began gulping that but, as with a light being switched off, let his head slump and soon began snoring, his right hand still clutching the cold bottle, condensation clinging lovingly to its sides and dripping over his knuckles. Rosa, smiling, walked swiftly up to him, and deftly prised the vessel from his fingers, before arranging his head to rest on a cushion. He was half lying down, his arms crossed almost like a baby, completely unconscious.

'Do you need to sleep too?' asked Rosa, turning to Johnny. She had moved a dining chair up close to him, as he sat next to the slumbering Pablo on the settee. He looked at her. She really was beautiful; with dark, darting intelligent eyes, high cheek bones and symmetrical face, long wavy black hair that she loved to throw back with an exaggerated gesture. Her figure was lithe and athletic; girly and tomboyish all at the same time. Johnny smiled; he knew his smile was honest and engaging, and he knew his blue eyes generated affection, but he was never satisfied with his looks. He wanted the short-long, straight hair style of a Mod, like Paul Weller, but his hair came out wavy, so he had to keep it short. And while women liked him, sometimes it was with a motherly, concerned air. He was handsome but not dangerous.

'I will need some sleep, but not yet. I slept more on the 'plane than Pablo. He was drinking all these coffees, watching the bad movies. I love this view!' he said, switching rapidly to look out of the window, and not at Rosa.

'Yes! You can only just make out the mountains because of the smog. But when it rains this time of year, the air clears, and it falls as snow up on the cordillera, so you have this amazing view of peaks and whiteness, like a beautiful ghost watching over you.'

'Beautiful. Let's hope it rains,' he said. 'What are the plans for the next couple of days?'

'Tomorrow you guys will just need to rest. Wednesday is the match. I have four tickets. For us three and for Nacho, a cousin; Pablo won't have seen him since he left, and won't remember him. He's like really old, 40 or something, but really cool.

There was a silence between them, deepening as the music finished. She got up wordlessly, walked barefoot, silent across the polished wooden floor, changed the CD. The smooth merengue tones of the Juan Luis Guerra album began. Rosa took Johnny by the hand. 'Now, you have to learn to dance.'

Johnny followed tentatively. 'Come on!' she insisted. 'I'll teach you to move your hips.'

She instructed him on the basic steps and they began to dance, Johnny excited and slightly unnerved by their closeness. 'Move your hips!' she said. '*Un poco mas*! Ah! *Los gringos no pueden bailar.*'

'What's that?' he asked.

'Gringos can't dance. But here, *mira*, I'll show you.'

She leant forward and placed her hands on his hips, encouraging them to move more exaggeratedly with each swing of the beat, as he stumbled his way through the steps, all the while she was singing throatily along, word- and note-perfect, to the hit song *Burbujas de Amor*. Johnny looked nervously up at Pablo, who was snoring with mouth open, head back on the sofa's back cushion, arms now outstretched, feet on the floor. Her hips moved in closer to his, one delicate but firm hand on his back, the other in his hand.

'I'm bad at this,' he apologised.

'Yes, but you're bad in a good way. You have natural rhythm,' she replied generously, her hand slipping briefly down to his waist.

'Thank you.'

The music changed to the next track, Pablo stirred, stretched his arms, half-opened his eyes. Johnny darted to the available seat. 'You're awake,' he began.

'It's cool mate, gringos should learn to dance.'

Johnny stared at him. Pablo closed his eyes again. Rosa stood with a puzzled look, like a mother watching over her twins who shared a secret language.

'Listen, you two. Why don't you go to bed properly? We can do fun stuff tomorrow!'

'ALL-SEATER STADIUM,' observed Johnny approvingly, as they took their places on the smooth grey plastic benches in the Estadio Monumental, in a southern suburb of Santiago. 'We still have standing terraces at Elland Road.'

'That's all going to end,' said Pablo.

'I will kind of miss it, mind. The singing, the surges when we get a goal.'

'It's a bit 19th Century.'

They were a good hour before kick-off. Johnny was at one end of the row of friends, Pablo next to him, then Rosa and Ignacio at the far end, for the pragmatic reason that he spoke very little English. The three lads were nervous; Rosa, thrilled and confident, declared: 'We will win 3-0. All goals by Barticciotto! I looooove him!'

'He's Argentinian,' protested Pablo. 'I want Chilean goalscorers!'

After little more than a quarter of an hour, a dreadful slip by an Olimpia defender let in the agile striker Luis Pérez for his second goal of the night, and there was little doubt from that moment on about the result. Rosa's prediction and Pablo's wish were fulfilled: a 3-0 result, with scorers of Chilean nationality; Barticciotto contributed with the assist for the third. Johnny, caught up in the passion of the 66,000-strong crowd, found he was as keen a supporter of Colo Colo as anyone.

The atmosphere was beyond euphoric on the way home, as they

drifted away to the bus-stops in the cool night air. Groups of people were jumping, dancing and singing, waving huge white flags. Already, horns were blaring as vans, buses and cars began careering around the nearby streets, fans hanging out of the windows, cheering and waving banners, the large white flags sporting the profile of the native American chief, symbol of the club; and smaller, black-and-white pennants. The fiesta was extending to the whole city. The four of them reached a crowded bus and Johnny ascended, helping Rosa up, grabbing onto her Colo Colo shirt to help her safely on. She gratefully clutched his upper arm with both hands, leaning in to avoid falling back out. They turned to look at Pablo and Nacho as the two of them attempted to get on, but they lost their balance and the bus began to move. Neatly jumping back off onto the pavement and avoiding injury, Pablo called out: 'We'll get the next one!'

Rosa called back: 'See you at the hotel!'

'What's it called again?' asked Pablo.

'Libertador! Appropriate!' She turned to Johnny. 'Run by an associate of my Dad. Should be a great party tonight. It's in the centre near the Metropolitan Park.'

'I'm not sure he heard you,' said Johnny, suddenly worried about his friend, almost as unfamiliar in the city as he was himself, though with the older Ignacio as his guide.

'That's all right. I'm sure I told him, and Nacho. They'll be fine. Wow, what a result! Amaaaazing! We won! We won! First Chilean team to win the Libertadores! Ever! Ha! I can't believe it! And we were there! Boy are we going to have a party. Tonight, Johnny, you are going to see Latin America at its most Latin American! *Vamos Colo Colo! Campeones!*'

The rest of the bus picked up her cue, singing '*Campeones, campeones!*'

Rosa, utterly nerveless in male company, continued to lead the singing. The bus swerved sharply around a bend. She clutched Johnny's biceps all the tighter with both her hands, and they tensed with pleasure in response.

Pablo and Ignacio did not make it to the hotel. Johnny and Rosa, secretly relieved at having time to themselves, glanced occasionally at the entrance. The first floor bar, with a view over Avenida O'Higgins, was buzzing but, this being an upmarket hotel, with less of the riotous clamour of the streets and the popular bars. Eventually Rosa declared: 'They'll have gone to Nacho's parents. They live on Avenida Madrid, just off Matta.'

'Where's that?'

'About half way between here and the stadium. I know the number. I'll call.'

He followed her to a bank of payphones on the first floor landing. 'No answer,' she said. 'Must be no one in. Or there could be so many partying that they can't hear the phone. I'll try again.'

She tried again, and again. Eventually Johnny could hear her chatting away, though of course was unable to understand. After a couple of minutes, she hung up, looking relieved.

'They're there all right. I spoke with Nacho. I asked to talk to Pablo but he said he's too drunk. I said he had better look after him, and they'd better stay there.'

'That's good. Everyone safe.'

'Yes,' she said. 'Shall we head back to the apartment?'

'Sure. Does the metro go near your street?'

'Yes, really close.'

'Shall we try that?'

'Don't want to risk it. Too many *borrachos* by this hour. Not so much fun when you're a woman,' she pulled a face. 'We'll try a cab.' The hotel could only offer a one-hour wait. They tried on the street but it was hopeless. The relentless procession of vans and cars, hooting, with fans leaning out of the windows, showed no sign of letting up. 'It's not raining. Let's walk,' she said.

'How far is it?'

'Couple of kilometres.'

They began the walk along the straight wide boulevard. Johnny adopted a steady gait, gazing with fascination at the street fiestas erupting all around him; Rosa alternated between walking, skipping and jumping, buzzing with as much energy as during the match in the stadium. Every time a car full of fans drove by, the occupants cheering as they leant out of the windows, Rosa waved back, cheering equally volubly, sometimes jumping up and down. As the crowds thinned out a little, she slowed her pace, and they walked side by side in silence for a while.

Johnny, desperate to disguise his desire, asked: 'You must be looking forward to Arturo returning to Santiago,' he said, diplomatically.

She grimaced.

'Sorry. Things not good between you?'

'Oh, I don't know. I love him, just maybe not as much as when we were 14. He used to be more romantic, when we were in our teens. Now all he seems to care about is *plata*.' She rubbed her forefinger and middle finger against her thumb as she uttered the word 'plata' with a world-weary air, rendering translation unnecessary.

'Pablo says you two were always destined to be together.'

'Oh yes, *si*, since we were seven, and walked down the aisle together.'

'*What?* You had a pretend wedding at age *seven*?'

'It's called First Communion. The girls get to dress in little white dresses to walk down the aisle to take the host for the first time, and we're paired up with a nice boy. It was always me and Arturo; Rosa and Arturo. Our parents were such close friends – *are* close friends – and Arturo and me were like three weeks apart in age.'

'I didn't know the Catholics had arranged marriages.'

'It's not called that, but all the Moms look at you and say how cute you look together. Could be worse. I mean, I do love him, I just want him to grow up. And be more like he was ten years ago.'

'Bit of a contradiction?'

'I'm hoping it's just a phase young men have, this only caring about careers and cars and money. Sometimes I feel like just an apparatus. You know, he has this machine for driving, this one for babies.

But I suppose at least we'll have a big house and a fucking swimming pool.'

Johnny looked up, mildly shocked by the cynicism and the expletive, wondering if she were fully aware of its impact within the English language. 'You shouldn't marry someone you don't love.'

'But I do love him, or at least how he was, and how he will be again. I don't know, we'll see. Now, where are we? Ah, not far now. Half a kilometre.'

The broad avenue was still busy with traffic at the late hour, but fewer of the vehicle occupants celebrating Colo Colo's historic victory, as they moved closer to the villas and gated driveways of Las Condes.

'Do you have a girlfriend?' she asked.

'No.'

'You will have a girlfriend very soon, and she will be very lucky.' She moved in again close to him, clutching his arm.

'Thank you,' he replied, not daring to say anything more. He wanted her physical closeness to continue, and to end, in equal measure. They were silent for a few hundred metres, and he was aware of how rare that was for her. He was also aware of her resting her head gently against his shoulder as they walked the last few yards, before detaching herself to find her key, and let themselves into the apartment block.

'I'm not tired!' she exclaimed as they entered the flat. 'Do you want a coffee, or a beer? I'm going to have a beer.'

'Me too,' said Johnny. 'I'm not drunk.'

'First, I take a shower and change. You relax. Play a CD. Or, play the guitar! That's a better idea!' she pointed towards the classical, nylon-stringed instrument, parked in the corner. Johnny picked it up and began to tune up.

After a few minutes she returned to the main room, having changed out of her Colo Colo shirt and jeans, into a short skirt and loose-fitting white blouse, with a token three or four of the buttons applied. Her mouth sported freshly applied lipstick, and she smiled broadly as she walked leisurely, barefoot, across the smooth wooden floor of the apartment, clutching a beer bottle in her left hand, listening to Johnny strumming the guitar.

'Play me a Beatles song,' she said.

'OK,' he replied. 'This one is especially suitable for today, after our conversation, walking back from the city.'

He began strumming. 'I don't know it!' she exclaimed, annoyed and thrilled in equal measure. He was sat cross-legged on the rug in the middle of the floor. She sat down in the same manner, directly facing him, a foot away. 'Start singing!' she instructed. He did so, and she began to hum along. 'Yes, I think I know the tune.'

'It's from A Hard Day's Night – the album. It's not on the movie.'

'Ah, that's why I don't know it so well. It's beautiful, *super-liiindo!* I love the way it's happy and sad, both at the same time.' She picked the tune up quickly, and by the end of the song could join in with the refrain: 'Things We Said Today'.

'We have said so much today,' said Johnny, tenderly, after he finished, the guitar lying face upwards on his lap.

'Those moments in that song,' she said. 'What *is* that? That feeling, in music?'

'What?'

'That moment where the tune is so right. It surprises you, yet you expect it at the same time. It is like the composer has read your thoughts, and it lifts you up; heavenly.'

Johnny found her choice of words startling – expressions in a second language can be more vivid, penetrating. For a moment he was unsure how to respond, then simply said: 'Only music can do that; lift you up.'

'I wish you could stay longer,' she said. 'I love your accent, I love your guitar playing.' She took a deep inward breath, and looked at him directly, deeply. 'Do you think that people who cannot sing or write poetry feel as much as those who do?' she asked. 'As much love, as much tenderness, as much — *como se dice* — fellow feeling, as much, anything?'

Johnny was silent for a while, caught unawares by the nature of the question. 'I don't see why not. Your sensitivity doesn't depend on talent, does it?'

'I'm sure they don't feel as much,' she said, with confidence. 'They can't feel as much as me, or as you. I'm sure of it.'

She pulled the guitar out from his lap, placing it carefully on the floor to one side of them. She looked him in the eye. She shuffled, still sitting cross-legged, over towards him. She leant forward, slightly, with a gesture so small it was huge.

The warning signs had flashed, long past code red. But Rosa had drawn him in, and her will was sovereign. Her brown eyes dazzled with darkness and with light, penetrated with desire. She leaned forward, kissed him wetly on the cheek and then, after a delicious pause, briefly on the mouth. She lifted her hands to caress both cheeks, gently. She leant forward further, and began to kiss him again. She moved her arms behind his neck to pull him in closer still. She moved one of her hands down the top of his spine, underneath his shirt.

Johnny paused in his movements, aroused and frozen, briefly pulling away but holding her gaze. Would the exhilaration of a few hours, of a magical night, of connecting with Rosa, of knowing her deeply, of pleasuring her repeatedly, of concluding their heavenly evening, having shared with a newly liberated people a night of un-bordered exultation, be worth the lingering fear of the terrible retribution he may face, as he cuckolded a rich and powerful young man, closely connected to the most fearsomely ruthless and intelligently directed despot of the western world, with a loyal armed forces still at his personal command?

It was not a difficult choice. Johnny returned her kiss. His hands reached over her cheeks and shoulder, down to her breasts, first through the light fabric of her blouse, then inside. She moaned with pleasure and pulled him further and further in, as he undid those few buttons that she had fastened in her bedroom, just a few minutes earlier. She stood up, took his hand and encouraged him up too, and guided him slowly but determinedly towards her room.

He hadn't imagined that it was possible for lovemaking to be tender and exciting, comforting and dangerous, all at the same time. She anchored him in his own self, while taking him to new territory. Their love was both discovered and made, created together yet with a sensation that it had always lain there, waiting to be uncovered. Lust is physical, but love even more so; rooted deep, deep in the body. This love could never be un-made, for the rest of their lives. This awareness filled them with ecstasy and despair, as they awoke, delirious but fragile, emerging into a different world. Regret was their only option. The regret of continuing; the regret of ending; with nothing more than the bittersweet joy of remembrance, and nothing less.

It was a sharp sound that had awoken them. The raps on the door bore a stronger opinion than a voice; four of them, then a pause, then five more.

'That'll be Pablo,' she said. 'About time.' She got up smartly, put on a bathrobe, pattered quickly down the wooden polished corridor. Johnny heard her open the door. 'Papa!' she said, terrified but trying to sound pleased. Johnny's nervous system froze, then his body. His eyes opened wider than they had ever managed before. He sat up.

BEFORE YOU GO

The book you are holding in your hand is the result of our dreams to be authors. We hope you enjoyed our stories as much as we enjoyed writing them. They exist through dedication, passion and love. Reviews help persuade readers to give this book a shot. You are helping the community discover and support new writing. It will take *less than a minute* and can be *just a line* to say what you liked or didn't. Please leave us a review wherever you bought this book from. A big thank you. On behalf of all our authors, the *Breakthrough Books* collective.

About the Authors

Stephanie Bretherton is an author and copywriter with a passion for the power of words, nature and science. A lifelong nomad and storyteller (in one medium or another) she now lives on a cliff in far west Cornwall. Her well-received, Kindle-bestselling novel *Bone Lines* will soon be followed by book two in *The Children of Sarah* series.
www.stephaniebretherton.com

Jamie Chipperfield is a full-time carer currently living in Cornwall. This anthology is his first time in print.
Twitter: @jchipperfield3

Sue Clark feels she's found her true calling as a writer of contemporary comic fiction, after a varied career as a BBC comedy scriptwriter, journalist, copywriter, editor and PR. Her debut novel, *Note to Boy*, was published in 2020. Her second, *A Novel Solution*, will appear in the near future.
www.sueclarkauthor.com
Twitter: @sueclarkauthor

Jason Cobley was born in Devon of Welsh parents. He is now an over-caffeinated teacher with high blood pressure and a few books to his name. This includes *A Hundred Years to Arras*, a pastoral war novel set in France in 1917. He now lives and ruminates in Warwickshire.
jmcobley.wordpress.com

Twitter: @JasonMCobley

Stevyn Colgan is an artist, musician, speaker, lecturer and author of ten books. He was, for a decade, one of the primary writers of the BBC TV show 'QI' and was on the writing team that won the Rose D'Or for Radio 4's 'The Museum of Curiosity'.

Samuel Dodson is an award-winning writer and editor based in London, UK. He is the founder of creative collective Nothing in the Rulebook. His first book, *Philosophers' Dogs*, was published by Unbound in 2021.
www.samuel-dodson.com
Twitter: @instantidealism

A.B. Kyazze is an author and photographer who worked around the world before settling in London. She has published many short stories and two novels, *Into the Mouth of the Lion* (2021) and *Ahead of the Shadows* (2022). A third novel is due out in September 2023. She also runs creative workshops exploring the senses, and is a Trustee for a fantasy writing charity.
www.abkyazze.com

Virginia Moffatt has written two novels *Echo Hall* (Unbound) and *The Wave* ((Harper One More Chapter) and a flash fiction collection *Rapture and What Comes After* (Gumbo Press). She is currently working on a couple of new novels and a novella. She lives in Dorset with her husband Chris.

Ivy Ngeow was born and raised in Johor Bahru, Malaysia. She holds an MA in Writing from Middlesex University. An author of psychological thrillers and literary short stories, her fifth and latest novel will be published by Penguin Books. She lives in London and is writing her sixth novel.
Free book here: tinyurl.com/freebookbyivy

www.writengeow.com
Twitter/instagram: @ivyngeow

Maybe because he's from Ireland, **Eamon Somers** loves writing stories with unreliable narrators. He says they often reveal more of life's truths than their more respectable cousin narrators. His debut novel *Dolly Considine's Hotel* clearly shows that Eamon has form in the area of lies and gross exaggeration.
eamonsomers.com

Paul Waters is the author of the crime thriller *Blackwatertown*. He's an award-winning BBC producer, co-hosts the award-winning *We'd Like A Word* books and authors podcast, and organises the *Chiltern Kills* crime fiction and *Khushwant Singh Litfest London* festivals. From Belfast, he was a radio reporter around the world. He taught in Poland, was a night club cook in New York, smuggled a satellite dish into Cuba, ran a G8 Summit in a South African township and made Pelé his dinner. He's either in Buckinghamshire or India.
www.paulwatersauthor.com

PJ Whiteley is an author of fiction and non-fiction. *Close of Play*, his first novel, received a review by the Church Times which stated that it was 'well written, but above all, well observed', while the follow-up *Marching on Together* received a cover quote from Louis de Bernières. *A Love of Two Halves* was described by SJ Bradley, editor of the literary journal *Strix*, as 'an uplifting northern novel'.
www.pjwhiteley.com

Acknowledgments

They say writing is a lonely art. We in the *Breakthrough Books* collective would disagree. Through the collective, we've been able to support each other and enjoy spending time with others who share our passion. But put a number of writers together and, inevitably, they write. The result is this collection of short stories. While we all played our parts, the book would not exist without the skill, hard work and, it has to be admitted, a certain amount of polite hassling of a trio of talents – Zena Barrie, Stephanie Bretherton and Ivy Ngeow. Thank you.

Printed in Great Britain
by Amazon